Without Words

Lisa Gurine

Introduction

As I put this pencil to paper and begin writing these words with my arthritic fingers, I feel nervous and uncomfortable. You see, I'm like the pendulum of that old grandfather clock that sits in the corner of my living room. It has been continually swinging back and forth and goes almost without notice. The clock marks time but is rarely thought about by those who surround it, and yet it persists faithfully and without complaint. One doesn't really need a clock, but nevertheless, it is there. On these pages I plan to record stories about the people and events that shaped my life. I have never shared these things with anyone, but a surprisingly persistent nudge from a place deep inside compels me to begin this project—pointless though it may be.

As I sit in my little house, I look out on this very brown December day. My home on this prairie may be small, but it's more than perfect for me. I am fortunate to have it. Thinking about those who constructed it brings me such comfort. Very little of its structure has changed since it was built all those years ago.

Though you wouldn't know to look at it, it's actually a sod house. The earthen bricks were harvested from this very land. I watched as the walls took shape. The wooden framing and plastered walls were added later to cover the original sod, which now acts as a wonderful insulation against the South Dakota cold.

Over the years our little town has grown and receded. It, and I, have survived two World Wars, the Great Depression, and the Korean War. Now our soldiers are fighting in the Vietnamese jungles as young people protest in the streets of big cities far from here. The stories of the world are not for me to write, though. Those conflicts I read about in the newspaper have little to do with day-to-day life in the farmlands of north central South Dakota. The stories swimming around in my head are much less dramatic and much more personal.

The good Lord Himself must be urging me to document these memories, but I can't say I understand what purpose will be served. I wonder, who will even read this? As I write, I imagine some stranger stumbling across these pages after I'm gone.

So, dear stranger, let me tell you about the events that shaped my existence. I'll start from as far back as I can remember.

My Beginning

My memories of my early childhood are scarce and disjointed. I remember the excitement in my mother's large brown eyes as she dressed me in a dainty, pink-flowered dress with cream ruffles at the hem and sleeves. Fabric, thread, and sewing supplies surrounded us, so she must have been making the garment just for me. Through the strands of her tousled, wavy brown hair, I saw the stick pins she held in her mouth as she told me to stand still. I marveled they did not fall to the floor. I wondered if she could feel them hit the tip of her nose as they bobbed up and down in her mouth. I believe I have the same nose—rather large and pointy with a slight downward curve at the tip.

When I started school, the other children made fun of my nose. They called me a dodo bird because I didn't speak and my nose resembled a beak. I suppose they thought that since dodo birds were extinct, they didn't make sounds. Funny how a child's mind creates these sorts of ideas. You might find it strange that I didn't mind the teasing. I liked to think my appearance was a gift from my mother—something she gave me so I could always see a part of her when I looked at my reflection in the mirror.

I must have been about two at the time my mother made me the dress, but I have no way of knowing for sure.

Next I remember the day we boarded the big boat. I was confused because we were carrying all of our belongings. I didn't understand that the ship would take us to an entirely different world—America. At the time, it just felt like an unfamiliar and wonderful adventure.

My father seemed very strong as he carried our things on board. His dark, curly hair was sticking to his sweaty forehead. He had a big, easy smile and quiet manner as he helped us board the ship. He wore a white linen shirt, unbuttoned at the neck. I could see his curly chest hair against his tan skin.

That brownish skin is another gift from my parents. When I'm outside in the garden a lot in the summer, I become very dark. Unlike others who live in these parts, I've never turned pink from the sun. In fact, some years I became so dark complected that a few gossiped about my being an Indian. Hulda squashed those rumors in a hurry.

My mother was all business once we'd boarded, securing a place for us to sit as she organized our trunks and bags. She immediately started talking excitedly to the other passengers, so my father and I were left to explore the ship. He was so curious. He opened doors and boxes and peeped in places that even then I knew we weren't allowed to see. One of the men working on the ship yelled at us to stop. Father scooped me up easily into his arms and carried me as he ran away through the crowds of people. We laughed as we made our way back to where we'd left my mother.

When we finally found her, she was sitting with an elderly couple eating plums. The three of them were just chatting away, discussing little, unimportant things like the weather and such. I remember the juice of the plums dripping down the man's chin, and I wondered why he didn't wipe it off. Then his wife took out a little handkerchief and dabbed it up for him without missing a word of the conversation. So comfortable they were with each other—the woman cleaning his face as nonchalantly as if it were her own, and the man not minding. That simple gesture has stuck with me as a beautiful expression of love.

My mother offered me a plum. Although my stomach was feeling a little queasy, I took it eagerly from her. I wanted to do what the grown ups were doing. I opened my mouth as wide as I could and took a big bite through the flesh and right into the pit. The sudden jolt I felt as my teeth hit the seed frightened me, and I spit the fruit onto the deck before I knew what I was doing. I thought I would be scolded for spitting, but when I looked up, I saw my mother, father, and the couple laughing. I laughed, too, even though I didn't understand the joke.

It all seemed so comfortable and normal at the time, but when I look back, I wonder about so many things. Did my parents know this couple, or did they just meet that day? Where did they get those plums? Were plums in season at the time? Did the elderly couple bring them on to the ship and share them with my mother, or did my mother bring the fruit and share it? Why plums, of all things?

I was so happy that day. Life seemed carefree and hopeful. It was a warm, sunny day and the salty sea air mixed with the scent of the plum juice smelled fresh and clean. One of the first things I did when I settled into my own little house was to plant a plum tree in the side yard. It has grown quite large now and produces enough plums to supply the whole town with as much jelly as they can put up. To this day, I think of my dear mother every time I smell the ripe plums in the fall.

Sadly, those brief snippets are all I have of my parents. Such insignificant moments, and yet for me, they are everything. You see, somehow after boarding the ship, after my father was so filled with adventure and my mother was savoring the sweet juices of the plums, I lost them. Both of them. Suddenly and forever. I know nothing more about either of them. They were just gone.

How I came to find Hulda and Herman, I don't know. I only know what I overheard them say about me later, which wasn't much. I don't know what happened to my parents or why Hulda couldn't find anyone who would claim me. I don't know where I'm from or how old I am. I don't even know my own name!

The closest thing I have to a name is Shadow. It's what everyone has called me as far back as I can remember. I don't particularly care for this name. I think it makes me sound more like a pet than a person. But that's what Hulda has called me since the very first, and that's what I have always answered to. Hulda told people that I followed her around the ship and hid under her bunk. She tried to shoo me away, but I always came back. Every time I appeared, Herman would say, "There's your little shadow again." So Hulda just began calling me Shadow.

When I overheard her tell the story, she said that she tried to find someone, anyone, who would claim me, but no one ever did. After the ship docked in Canada, she couldn't bring herself to leave me, especially because I clung so close to her. At this point in her story, she sighed and asked, "What choice did I have but to bring her along?"

Hulda wasn't happy to include me in their new life. She made no secret of that fact. She and Herman were expecting their first child, and I was more than a mere inconvenience to them. They had been married only a few months before their journey across the ocean and were planning to homestead before starting a family. Hulda always had a rigid plan for everything and was never happy when that plan needed to be altered. When she discovered she was going to have a baby so early in their marriage, she was upset. Herman, for his part, was happy at the thought he might have a son so soon after the wedding, but he was nervous about providing for a baby at the same time he would be buying land and building a home. I was an additional burden neither of them was prepared for. Oh, Hulda and Herman treated me well, and I am so grateful that I found them. Still, I've never been a part of their family, just more of a "Shadow." Always a step behind, always there but never noticed.

Part of the reason for this, of course, is that I don't talk. I'm not sure why. Hulda and Herman took me to a doctor once when I was about nine or ten years old. They were afraid I might have pnuemonia. The physician was so curious about my silence that he asked if he could perform some tests to discover the cause. When Hulda and Herman looked at each other with an uncomfortable hesitation, he added, "Free of charge, of course."

After his examination, he declared there was nothing wrong with my throat or vocal cords. My inability to speak was not physical but psychological. Perhaps I had suffered some sort of trauma on the ship, he surmised, so my being mute resulted from some sort of emotional breakdown. He called my condition "Selective Mutism." I have no opinion about all that. I know I could talk if I wanted to. I simply have never seen the point nor felt the need since I have never had anything important to contribute to a conversation. Through gestures and facial expressions, people have always understood me just fine. I can't even remember ever wanting to speak. Well, except for that one time. But I'll get to that later.

Because of my silence, my name suits me even if I don't care for it. I grew up in the shadows. I understood my place with these people, and I respected it. If I sat quietly, people would just forget I was there and go on about their day. I tried never to bother anyone. As time went on, people would sometimes seek me out to talk about their thoughts and feelings. They told me that I'm a good listener, that they can trust me. Those kind words always bring a smile to my face, but I don't quite understand why they feel this way. I only listen. Whether I'm particularly "good" at it or not is really beside the point. I listen. I don't help them, offer advice, or make any difference. I just listen. It's who I am, and it's all I know.

As I think about the stories I plan to write, I realize I have outlived almost everyone I ever knew. I guess that if it is truly God who has called me to put these memories on paper, I can do so without fear of betraying any confidence. Only one or two are left now who would even be able to question or correct me. Regardless of that fact, I promise to relate these tales to you as truthfully as I can. They come directly from my eyes, my mind, and my heart.

I can't imagine what good will come from this labor. How can a shadow be important? A shadow doesn't change the world or even matter. But I feel the Lord calling me, and for Him I will answer. Not with spoken words, but with written ones.

Theophil

Hulda told people she had been an American since 1881, so that must be the year I arrived here as well. It was the same year that she and Herman were married and the same year their first child, a boy, was born. They named him Valentine, but from the moment of his birth, everyone referred to him as Val. Hulda would often joke that her life saw more changes in that one year than in all the years before or since.

Most people arrived in America by way of New York and have memories of the Statue of Liberty. Our ship went to Canada first. I read once that many people went to Canada to avoid U.S. immigration laws and paperwork. The article said that before 1900, people from Canada could enter the U.S. without documentation. Perhaps that's why we landed in Canada: It was easier. Or, maybe I'm French and my parents were going to meet their relatives. A lot of French people settled in Canada. Over the years, I've been told that I look Italian or Greek. Some have even suggested that I'm a Jew. I've wondered, of course, but in the end, knowing wouldn't change anything.

Hulda and Herman were German. They were from a place called Odessa, Russia. Outside of this town in Russia was a village populated with Germans. Though it seems strange to say you are a German from Russia, there are a lot of German Russians around here. That's probably why we settled on this prairie. Hulda and

Herman knew people here, so it seemed like a logical place to go. People gravitate toward the familiar. In fact, a person walking into a crowded room will often take a chair close to someone they know and don't particularly like rather than risk sitting next to someone they don't know but might actually enjoy. Strange, isn't it?

As I have already told you, I was quite small when I got off of that ship. As I sit, now, at the little desk next to the picture window in my living room, I watch as the snow has started to gently fall and obscure the brown earth with its blanket of white. I realize that what I have always thought of as my memories of that time are more likely just a compilation of the memories and stories of others. So, because I have no choice, I will share with you what I have pieced together and adopted as my own history.

We landed in Canada. At some point we boarded a train and made our way down to America, halfway across the country to a town called Aberdeen in the Dakota Territories, now North Central South Dakota. The details about that train ride are lost somewhere deep in the recesses of my mind. In later years, Hulda sometimes laughed about her irrational fear of train travel. She'd begged Herman to walk instead of boarding such a death trap. She imagined the other passengers would all have guns and would be shooting without regard for the safety of others. Earlier that same month, President Garfield had been shot in a train station, and that was all Hulda knew about trains. Smiling, she described how hard it had been for Herman to convince her Dakota Territory was too far to get to by foot, especially in her condition.

Hulda was stubborn and seldom would anyone get her to change her mind once it was set on something. But, Herman, in his quiet, gentle manner, had a way of breaking through and convincing her to see things differently.

The train finally stopped in Aberdeen. Aberdeen became an official town the same year we arrived. It was named by one of the wealthy railroad owners, Alexander Mitchell, who was originally from Aberdeen, Scotland. Back then, most people still referred to the place by its nickname, the Hub City. There the tracks of the numerous railroads all met, coming together to a hub like the spokes of a wheel. Even today, most local people call it the Hub City.

It was a small town of only about 3,500 people when we arrrived. Yet it was the biggest community for more than a hundred miles in any direction. So many travelers making their connections to other trains made the city seem bigger than it was. The convergence of the rail lines created many opportunities for the new arrivals. There was construction on every corner, it seemed. Hotels, cafés, churches, bars, and every sort of business you might expect in a big city were being developed. Herman said he couldn't wait to get out of there. He sometimes referred to it as the 'Hive City' because all the people coming and going reminded him of a swarm of bees. He'd declare, "If I spent another minute in that tangled-up mess, I'd surely be stung!"

Once we got settled in our little community on the prairie, I didn't have much opportunity to go back to the city. It's hard to believe, but I've actually only been there about half a dozen times in my whole life. Going to the city seemed exciting when I was young, but after the first couple trips, I felt like Herman. There were just too many people, moving too fast in every direction. A place like that is enough to make your head spin.

Nowadays, in the 1960s, people get up in the morning and drive to Aberdeen, do their shopping, and return home in time for supper. Seems like a waste of a perfectly good day to me. We have everything we need in our little town, and here you don't have to worry about being stuck in a car all day or being surrounded by a bunch of strangers. But back then, you would have to make your way on foot, horseback, or wagon, and the trip could take almost a week. The trekking was slow going, so you would even need to sleep alongside the trail.

This place we live is a flat, treeless land. Except for all of the rocks, lack of water in the summer, and cold, harsh winters, it's a perfect place to farm. There's no need to spend a lot of time clearing a field. Just get out there, pick up the rocks, and you have yourself a place to plant. Many of us built rock fences and even reinforced the foundations of our barns and houses with them. Not a bad place to call home. Of course, it's the only place I have ever called home, so who am I to say?

Anyway, we moved along the trail to our settlement that first week in August 1881. The heat and humidity were stifling. The wind blew the dust from the dry prairie around relentlessly, and multitudes of grasshoppers jumped and scattered with every step.

At least we didn't travel alone. In Aberdeen, we met up with several others going the same direction. The walking was hard. Folks carried everything they owned on the backs of their animals or in wagons. Herman filled his small wagon with all of their things and the supplies he had gathered before leaving town. Although the wagon was heavily loaded, the two work horses he purchased seemed to pull it with ease. We walked alongside it. Hulda didn't move fast with the baby growing in her expanding stomach. She must have been so uncomfortable, but I don't ever recall her complaining except when Herman would demand we stop to take a rest. She didn't want to be the cause of the group delaying their arrival and would often argue that she was "just ducky" and didn't need a rest. Herman, to his credit, would insist that his shoulders were aching and he needed to put the pack down for a bit.

I wasn't much help to anyone, of course. In fact, I slowed Hulda and Herman down considerably. One day I overheard Hulda ask Herman if they should find a little farm along the way and leave me. Herman got really upset. I didn't like to see him get mad, and it scared me a little. He was so slow to anger that I knew it must be something really big for him to get that agitated.

I ran behind Hulda and grabbed one of her legs as tightly as I could. Herman was mad, and I wanted to hide from him. I didn't really understand what they were talking about, but I knew it was about me. All of a sudden they both started laughing, and Hulda picked me up. Her stomach was so big by this time that I sort of sat on top of it. She hugged me and said to Herman, "You're right of course. How could I leave my shadow? No matter how far I go or how fast I run, I will never lose my shadow."

I didn't know then what she was talking about, but I have remembered those words all these years. They gave me such comfort at the time. She said she could never outrun me, and I took that to mean I would never be abandoned. Later, as I replayed these words in my mind, I wondered if she wished she could have run fast enough to lose me.

On that trail is where I first met Theophil. He was around twenty years old when he left the old country to homestead. He made quite an impression on me when he first joined us.

The day before, while Hulda and I waited outside the train station for Herman to return with some supplies, I overheard a woman tell her little girl about a boy named Jack and a giant who lived at the top of a beanstalk. I had never heard a story so filled with fantasy like this before, and I couldn't get it out of my mind. When I first saw Theophil, I pretended that he was the giant from that story because he was so tall and had such big broad shoulders. After a bit, I let my imagination convince me that instead of a giant, he was actually the beanstalk because he was incredibly thin as well. Finally, I decided he must be Jack because his smiling light brown eyes always seemed to shine against his tanned face and dark brown hair. I pictured Jack looking just this way. But truthfully, probably the main reason I thought of that story when I saw him was because he walked with a cow. The whole way!

Later, I learned that he bought the cow in Canada and even paid for her to ride on the train. The cow rode in the cattle car with other livestock, and they said that Theophil would check on her at every stop. Since many animals died in the close quarters of the boxcars, Theophil may have been worried he had invested his money foolishly, even though she was a healthy animal. Luckily, the cattle wagon on Theophil's train had the new louvered slats on the sides that allowed air to pass through. He named the big, brown, dusty thing Lily and talked to her as if she were a person.

When I got tired and couldn't keep up with Hulda, Theophil sometimes let me ride on Lily. I didn't like it too much. Lily smelled bad, and she sure wasn't soft or comfortable to sit on. But it was so nice of him to let me ride on her. It helped everyone keep a good pace and assured me I wouldn't be left behind.

The flies on that cow were relentless. The buzzing and swarming around my ears and face almost made me crazy. One time I picked up my skirt and pulled it right over my head. I couldn't see anything, but I felt an instant relief from those pesky insects.

Before I knew what was happening, Hulda whipped me off that cow and gave me a good spanking. She said that a lady never lifts her skirt in front of men. I didn't understand. I wasn't "in front of men." I was just with Theophil, and he didn't care.

She told me she was ashamed of me and wished my mother had taught me manners. Then she said it was no wonder my mother had probably abandoned me, and if she had half her mind, she would, too.

I admit I cried that day and on many days after. I cried not because of the spanking but because of the words against my mother. I didn't know her, but I felt sure she taught me all of the good and decent things a mother should teach her daughter. It wasn't my mother's fault. It was mine. I was just absentminded and forgot her lessons. That's all. Hulda could be quite harsh when she was tired and hungry. She was both that day, and her words still sting even these many years after her death.

But let me tell you more about Theophil. He was the first person I considered my friend. The first time I saw him with that cow, I thought he was a strange man to talk to an animal like he did. Yet he had a quick smile and an easy manner. He walked with a rare self assurance that made you believe he would succeed in the new country. Everyone seemed to like him. When there was a question about which direction to go or how to fix one of the wagons, they always turned to Theophil. Sometimes someone would ask him something like, "What kind of supplies will there be when we get there?" Theophil would laugh and say, "Now, how would I know such a thing? I'm on this journey right alongside you, not?" He always ended a statement like that. He would say, "That sun sure is hot today, not?" or "That horse looks sick, not?"

As I imagined Theophil's playing each part in the Jack and the Beanstalk fairy tale that first day on trail, he caught me looking at him. I felt a bit starstruck when he walked right up to Hulda and said, "Who is this little princess you got here?"

Hulda said, "Oh that. That's just my shadow. She started following me around when we was on the boat, and I can't seem to shake her. Guess she's mine now and probably forever."

Theophil looked a bit pained at her comments right in front of me. But I was used to them. Plus, it isn't like they weren't true. I did follow her everywhere. I had nowhere else to go, and even if I did, I wouldn't have left her side to get there.

Theophil asked, "Well, what's her name, then? Where are her folks?"

Hulda said, "She ain't got no parents that I ever saw. She started following me when we was on the ship. I couldn't find anyone to claim her. And she don't talk, so I don't have any idea what her name is or what she's thinkin'. She seems to understand things, but I think she's a little slow or somethin'. Never a peep. Just a quiet little shadow."

Theophil looked me right in the eyes. Not many people ever really looked at me, but he always did. I think that's one of the things I loved best about him. He saw me. He said, "Well, now, little shadow, why don't you come and keep me and old Lily here company for a while?"

I was scared and didn't want to go with him. I really had never let Hulda out of my sight, and I didn't want to be out of arm's reach of her. I've often thought of those early days. I really was a pest to Hulda. I was so worried she would eventually leave me that I clung to her almost constantly. With an exhausted sigh, Hulda replied to Theophil, "That would be a relief! I'd much appreciate a bit of a break."

With a hard shove in my back from Hulda, I stumbled into the open arms of Theophil. That settled that. I walked with

Theophil and Lily most of the day. I soon learned I didn't have a thing to be frightened of, and I spent long hours walking beside them. The nice thing was, Theophil loved to talk. We were a perfect match. He talked, and I listened. His voice was deep, and he had a slow manner of speech. He seemed to think about each word before he spoke it, and yet he didn't stop talking. Because of the slow, rambling stories he told, others got tired of listening and moved along. But not me. I loved the way he spoke. If I close my eyes, I can almost hear him now. "Well, Shadow, it's getting dark. Time for bed, not?"

Theophil's favorite topic on that long walk was his fiancée back home. I don't recall him ever saying her name on that trip. He always said, "my fiancée back home." He added the "back home" to the "my fiancée" part each time he referred to her. One time a fella asked him, "Is 'back home' part of her first name, or is it her last name?"

Everyone around laughed, but I didn't. I could see that even though Theophil smiled and nodded as if he was in on the joke, he didn't really think it was one bit funny. He never let others know when he was annoyed or angry. He just always went along. I think that's one of the reasons people liked him so much. You have to admire someone who can control his temper and laugh at himself. It made him really easy to be around.

Theophil met his fiancée back home at church. His version of church anyway. See, Theophil called himself a Bible Student. He didn't go to church the way most people did. He and others like him believed the only "church" you needed was to study the Word of God, and that Word came in the form of the Bible. They would gather at each other's homes each week and read and discuss a verse or two of the Good Book. There would be assignments and other books to read that explained more about the verses. These students would often switch up their study groups so they could always get fresh thoughts and ideas.

Theophil read the Bible every day. No matter how early we needed to leave, Theophil would get up even earlier to read his verses. He told me it was the best way for him to start the day. He said, "If you talk to God first thing in the morning, the rest of your day will go just His way. His way is the best way to start a day, not?"

I sometimes got up and sat with him while he read. If I was there, he would read out loud, and I always felt so special to have someone reading quietly to me. I have to admit, though: I'm not the most diligent Bible Student. Even now, I often find I prefer sleep to the early morning Word of our Lord. I'm not only old, but I'm also weak.

It was at one of these weekly Bible meetings that Theophil first met his fiancée back home. He told me that he could hardly hear the words that were being spoken that night, and he sure couldn't read any of them. He said he was so taken with her beautiful eyes and shining brown hair that he could hardly speak. His face turned so red that first night that one of the women got him some cream thinking he had a sunburn!

Besides loving to talk, Theophil always told a good story, too. But sometimes he exaggerated things to get his point across. I love the thought, though. Just imagine how beautiful a woman would have to be to cause a man to look sunburned just by her mere presence. I wish I could have seen a picture of her.

Theophil was relentless in his pursuit. He said he found out where she lived, what she did for entertainment, and what her favorite flower was before the sun came up the next morning. He went to visit her twice a week with dandelions in hand. Now this seems a bit hard to believe, but it's what he told me on many occasions. The favorite flower of his fiancée back home was DANDELIONS! A weed!

Of course, dandelions covered the prairie, and he always seemed a bit melancholy when he picked one as we walked. He would pause and lift it to his face, inhaling the distinctive scent of the flower. There's something to be said for a woman who prefers something so simple, available, and easy to get. Maybe that's why she liked Theophil. He wasn't a complicated man, he made himself plenty available, and he sure didn't play hard to get.

When Theophil visited his fiancée back home, he always spent some time teasing her younger sister, Lydia. Lydia was a cute, energetic little thing with curly blonde hair and sparkly blue eyes. She was about five years younger than her sister and about eight years younger than Theophil. Lydia often accompanied Theophil and her sister on their outings. She went to picnics, fishing trips, and Bible meetings with them. Lydia loved to fish just like Theophil, and sometimes he would take her fishing, and they would spend the day alone talking and laughing together.

As I write about Theophil, it occurs to me that on that long walk, I heard a lot more about Lydia than I did her sister. Theophil always talked about how quiet, shy, and beautiful his fiancée back home was. He would go on and on about her smile or the way she tilted her head. He really never told me what they talked about, though, or what they had in common. That was where Lydia came in. Lydia was a jokester and always wanted to play a game or have an adventure. She was always coming up with some plan for the three of them and would lead them to all sorts of places.

Later, when we arrived in Dakota Territory, Theophil homesteaded the place right next to us. It was about a half mile walk from house to house, and over the next months and years, I spent a great deal of time with him. I helped him hang curtains on the little windows in his kitchen and sitting room. When trying to make a decorating decision, he would sometimes ask me things like which fabric he thought his fiancée back home would prefer. Or if he bought a plate, he would ask me, "Do you think she would like flowers or stripes better?" If he put a rug on the floor, he would ask, "You think she would want it laid horizontally or vertically?" I always pointed to the one I preferred, but I wondered if his fiancée back home would choose the same. I was having fun with Theophil, and I felt important, so I tried not to think about her too much.

Looking back, it's funny that he took such stock in the opinions of a little girl. But that's why I loved him. He treated me like a person, not like a child, or worse, like a shadow.

One spring day about two years later, Theophil said he had decided he was ready for his fiancée back home to join him. He had his second crop in the field and the house was as ready as it was going to be. Theophil had made some good friends, and he picked out the most beautiful spot on the prairie to have the wedding. The spot was on a little hill on the other side of his place. A giant cottonwood tree stood on the top of it, like a soldier watching over the fields. The cool shade that tree put off in the heat of the summer was nothing short of miraculous, and in the fall, the bright yellow leaves seemed to hold the sun itself in its branches. I really felt it was the perfect spot for a wedding. If they got married in the summer, I planned to collect as many dandelions as I could find for a big bouquet. I wanted her to like me. I didn't want to lose Theophil.

Theophil showed me the letter he wrote to her. He said that it would be the first letter they exchanged since he left. He explained that before he left, he told his fiancée back home of his plans to live in America. He asked for his beloved's hand and told her the next time she would hear from him would be when he had established himself in the New World. Theophil was romantic, and I think he liked the idea of this silent anticipation between them. I don't think he realized it would be more than two long years later, though.

I had just started attending school and learned to read quickly and easily. Ironic that I have such an aptitude for the written word even as I have no desire for the spoken word.

I struggled a bit to read his small and jagged cursive and had to point to a few of the bigger words that were unfamiliar to me. Theophil patiently explained their meaning so I would understand. The letter went something like this.

My Dearest Emma,

I am writing to you with a heart filled to the brim with joy and love. I am so excited that I feel I may jump right out of my own skin. Dearest, I am ready! Our waiting is over. I have finally managed to build the dream we always desired. We have a few acres of good soil. We have Lily, our cow, for milk and a few chickens for eggs. We have a couple pigs and a nice vegetable garden. My crops are doing well, and God willing, the weather will hold again this year for a nice harvest. The house is modest but well appointed. It is time to pack your trunk and join me for our beautiful life together in this wide-open land. Dearest, you can see for miles in every direction without a bump or bush to block your view. The sky is vast and the days are long. The labor is hard and makes me feel like I am working by the strength of the Lord alone. As full as my days are, I am lonely. I count the minutes until I can see your face. Hurry to me, my dearest. I am ready, and I am waiting!

> *With loving anticipation,*
> *Your Theophil*

Funny, but I felt a little hurt that he said he was lonely. I mean, I knew I didn't talk like other people, but I was over at his place almost every day. Then, I thought, it could be he felt sad when I went home to the family for supper and left him to eat alone. Eating can be lonely business. I vowed then that when I grew up, I wouldn't let the people I love eat every meal alone. Over the years, I regularly visited as many people as I could for breakfast, dinner, or supper. I don't get out too much anymore, but thankfully I have a good many people in this community who stop by to keep me company on occasion. I'm glad that I made the effort to pass some time with others when I was young because I really understand, now that I am old, how much it meant to them.

Despite that twinge of pain, I felt a thrill at hearing her name. *Emma.* It's a pretty name, and I liked that I could think of her as someone other than *Theophil's Fiancée Back Home.* I felt like I was in on a secret.

As I read the letter, Theophil watched me. He seemed to hold his breath until I finished. Then he asked, "It'll do the trick, not?" I smiled and nodded. Of course she would come immediately. Who wouldn't want to spend their days with him?

After about a week, Theophil started making the trip to town every other day to check for return mail. There was no way the letter could have arrived in Odessa in just a week, much less that he would get a return post that quickly. But I understood how anxious he was.

Theophil wanted everything to be perfect for Emma's arrival. He swept the floor every morning and shook out the rugs every night. There wasn't a dish out of place or a weed to be found in the garden. I don't know where he found the time. He also had the biggest pile of wood in the whole township. Some of the men joked that he was working his frustrations out, and they would elbow each other and laugh. Theophil would smile and nod, but I could tell he didn't think it was one bit funny.

Weeks turned into a month and then two without word. Theophil started to speculate that the letter never made it to his fiancée back home or that maybe she was on her way and was going to try and surprise him. He also worried that maybe she was sick or hurt. The poor man's emotions were all over the place. He was near tears one second, and the next he was peering off in the distance asking if I thought that looked like a wagon coming this way. I ate supper with him a few nights a week during that time. I think it helped for him to express his thoughts out loud. I prayed every night that she would send a letter. I couldn't imagine what took her so long.

One day I went over to his place before breakfast. Hulda, now with two young boys and another on the way, had run short of eggs, and she wanted me to see if Theophil could spare some. He had quite a few chickens and often had more eggs than he could eat by himself, so she knew he wouldn't mind.

When I walked in, I found him ironing his nightclothes. He was pressing them to get every wrinkle out. As I watched him, he seemed a bit embarrassed and mumbled, "Today could be the day, not?" He folded that nightshirt as neat as any washer woman ever could and placed it underneath his pillow. He wanted to be ready for his fiancée back home to appear at any moment and obsessed about every detail. It was so important to him that he present a good first impression of their home to her.

I worried that she might not like me. People talked about how strange I was. They sometimes said so right in front of me as if they thought that since I couldn't speak, I couldn't hear, either. Not talking seemed to be unsettling to some. Smaller children were even a bit scared of me at times. I never could figure out why. To me, the less noise and ruckus a person makes, the less scary he is. But, as young as I was, I realized I wasn't the kind of person everyone liked straightaway, and I worried that if his fiancée back home didn't like me, my days of having Theophil for a friend would be over.

After four long months, on a beautiful September afternoon, Theophil came back from the post office with a letter in his hand. He was smiling bigger than I have ever seen anyone smile before. He came right up to our house and asked Hulda if I could join him for supper that night. Of course, Hulda said, "What a relief to have one less mouth to feed mouth around here!" That was her way of saying I could go with him.

On the way to his house he showed me the letter. Since I had sat with him during his long wait, he said, the least he could do was let me share in his joy. We sat down to supper, and after the dishes were washed, he said, "It's time to see what she says, not?"

You see, he was so excited for this letter that once he had it in his hands, he wanted to wait until the perfect moment to savor it. I was so happy for him. My stomach was jumping all over the place. I wanted to rip that letter open and read it for myself. I thought, "YES, Theophil, yes, it's time!"

We sat down in the little parlor area just off the kitchen, and he opened the letter. He started to read it out loud in a strong, happy voice. That long-awaited message was stunningly brief.

Dear Theophil,

I fear I have somehow misled you. We did have some nice times all those years ago, but those time are in the past. As I recall, you asked for my hand in marriage, and then you left before I could answer. I feel sick to tell you that my answer was no. I have moved on. I do not desire the life you have to offer. In truth, I never did. My sister, Lydia, is the one who loves adventure, not me.

With fondness for the past,
Emma

As young as I was, I was immediately aware of the pain that note held. Even all these many years later, it brings tears to my eyes to think of the hurt that man suffered from those few words. The sobs started deep in his chest and came out slow and heavy with each breath. Almost as if the air was being forced right out of his lungs. He started crying and sobbing. Never before or since have I seen a man show such raw emotion.

I ran to him and hugged his knees. Tears streamed down my own face. I was crying as hard as he. This man I loved. My friend. The first person who ever really saw me was hurting from a pain so deep and so real that I couldn't imagine it would ever subside. Theophil felt lost, lonely, unloved, and most of all foolish and betrayed. We cried together that night for a long time. It was very late and past time for me to go home. He hadn't moved from the position he was in when he finished the letter. He couldn't move. He couldn't talk. He had cried so much that he sobbed now without tears. This pain was physical, unstoppable.

I finally walked home in the dark. When I got there, Hulda was ready for me. I didn't usually stay out so late, and even though she was mad, she was worried, too. It made me feel bad for causing her to be so angry, but it also made me feel a little good. Kinda like maybe she loved me a little. Like maybe I was more than just a shadow always following her around.

Anyway, she took one look at my swollen red eyes and knew something bad had happened. She kept yelling at me to tell her what was wrong, but all I could do was cry and point to Theophil's place.

Finally Herman stepped in. He said, "Did something happen over at Theophil's?"

I nodded.

Then, he asked, "Is he hurt?"

I nodded again. With the little boys and baby asleep in their beds, both Hulda and Herman bolted out of the house and ran to Theophil's place with no regard for the late hour. I ran after them. I didn't know what else to do.

They found him just as I had left him. Crying without tears. Those big, deep, breathy sobs. He clutched the letter in his hands and didn't speak. Hulda pried the letter from his fists and read it out loud to Herman. The pain we all felt for him was thick in the room. Theophil looked down at his feet as if he was ashamed. As if somehow he had done something to cause this. I had to imagine what he was thinking and feeling because, for the first time since I met him, he refused to talk.

That was the start of Theophil's deep darkness. He could barely speak about it, and he tried to say as little as possible about anything else. He sat in his chair and rocked slightly back and forth without making a sound. One day, I stopped over and found that he had put the letter on the mantel of the fireplace in his parlor. He had it propped up there like a show piece. I didn't know if he was staring at the letter or the fire as he rocked. Maybe both.

The neighbors, both men and women, tried to reason with him. They prodded him to chop some wood or pick the vegetables that were starting to rot in his garden. But he just couldn't make himself move.

One day, Hulda came to me with tears in her eyes. "Shadow, I'm at my wit's end with that man. You have a special friendship with Theophil. Go over there and see if you can convince him to start living again. Somethin's got to be done. He can't go on like this."

I really didn't know what to think. On the one hand, I felt honored that she saw me as someone special—even if only special to someone else, not her. I also felt really proud that she thought I could help. To Hulda, I had always been an unwanted burden she was forced to carry. Now maybe she would see me as a person who had value. Someone who could be called upon in times of trouble. As bad as I felt for Theophil—and believe me, I felt bad— I also felt really hopeful for myself.

That feeling didn't last long. I was just a little girl. A girl who didn't talk. My only skill was listening, and when the person I was trying to help didn't talk either, not much got done. Every morning I went over to his house, and I stayed by his side until after supper every night. He didn't say much. Sometimes he cried a little. A few times he held my hand. The neighbors came and went. Hulda was very disappointed in me. During that time, I was nothing more than Theophil's shadow. I wished so hard I could be someone else. Someone who could matter to someone else. But it wasn't my time, and I wasn't any help.

Theophil started to lose weight. He was tall and thin to begin with, so any weight he lost or gained was obvious right away. After a couple of weeks, his cheeks began to sink in a little, and his arms looked like bones covered in skin. Nothing more. The women of the area started bringing him food. At first they brought hearty meals. Meals made for hungry men. Chicken and dumplings, roast beef and potatoes, stews of all sorts, pies and pastries of all types. But it seemed the only thing they could get into him those first few days was brothy soup. If Theophil could sip it from a cup, he would take the nourishment. If he had to hold a knife and fork and eat from the table, forget it. He didn't want to leave that chair by the fireplace, and he refused to break his gaze from the letter (or maybe the fire).

While the women nursed him, the men worked his land. Because of his hard work that spring and summer, his crops were the best for miles around. His farm was the envy of the entire township. It seemed everything he planted produced a bounty like no other. Theophil had worked so hard to make everything perfect for his fiancée back home, and the time had come to reap the rewards of that labor. The trouble was, Theophil wouldn't leave that chair. When his friends tried to convince him to start working again, he just shrugged his shoulders and asked, "What for?" When they told him he needed fresh air and sunshine, he said, "No point." Someone told him he needed to think about living again.

He turned his head from the letter and said, "Why?" Then turned his eyes back to where they had been resting and didn't say anything more the rest of the day.

No one knew what to do with him. He refused to be consoled. It really was wonderful the way the people of the township gathered around him. I was amazed at how quickly Hulda organized everyone. She was an incredible woman with a mind for getting things done. She made a chart, and that first Sunday after the letter arrived, she made everyone sign up for something after church. One would bring him breakfast and pick the eggs. Another would bring lunch and pick the garden vegetables. Someone else would bring supper and chop some wood. The neighbors all took shifts working to bring in his crops.

As autumn turned to winter, these people gathered around Theophil to help him without asking for a thing in return, even though they had their own little ones to care for, their own livestock to feed, and their own cows to milk. When times are tough, good people come around and do what they can to help.

We often hear about how selfish humans can be. Well, that fall and winter, I didn't observe selfishness. I observed strength, perseverance, friendship, and selfless love. Some of the people who did the most work hardly knew Theophil before that letter. They had no reason to make such sacrifices. But they did! It warms my heart to think of it.

One night, the snow came down hard. It snowed at least half a foot and maybe more that night. The wind came up, and the drifts were high. I got up early and headed over to Theophil's because I was sure the woman who was signed up for the breakfast shift wouldn't make it. I didn't want Theophil to be alone all day. It took all my strength to buck that wind to cross our yards. When I walked in that house, what did I find? The breakfast woman was already there with the coffee on and muffins in the oven. She must have gotten up in the middle of the night to make it there. She was humming a little tune and didn't let on for a minute how tired and worn out she was. I could see it in her eyes, but if I didn't look close, I could see only her soft, sweet smile. I was so happy that others saw the good in Theophil that I saw.

As I sit here now in my rocking chair by the fire, watching the flames dance in the late afternoon light and reflect on those people long ago, my heart glows. The generosity of their spirit overwhelms me. Maybe my perspective has changed with age, but I think people were just plain better back then.

As good as people are, they get tired or bored or just need a break. As winter started to wear thin that year, the help stopped coming so often. The cheerful, kind words turned into deep sighs and exasperated looks. Theophil was in a bad place, and people could only take it so long. I don't blame them; they really gave all they had in them to give. He just seemed to need so much. I heard people say it was time for him to be getting over it. That he'd sat around long enough and that now he was taking advantage of them.

Unlike me, these people didn't understand that Theophil had spent years preparing for a life that was no longer going to be his. He lost more than his fiancée back home; he lost the future he had dreamed of for so long. Every breath he took and every thing he did was all to get him closer to that dream. It was all taken from him. With just a few short sentences, he was set adrift with no plan and a life without meaning.

Spring came that year all at once. It was cold one day and then the next, southerly winds started to blow, and it was warm. Really warm. The heat of the sun stayed, and a slow warm rain followed. The snow was completely gone within in a week. Usually when the snow melts in spring, we get another winter storm, or maybe two or three more. The snow melts and tricks us into believing spring is here, and then it turns cold and snows again. Mother Nature laughs that she fooled us yet another time. But that year, it was cold one week, and the next week it was spring. No trick. Spring was here, and it felt wonderful to breathe the fresh outdoor air again.

One afternoon in that unseasonably warm April, I sat just breathing in the sunshine on Theophil's hill under his cottonwood tree (it's still there to this day). The leaves were already starting to bud. I imagined how beautiful Theophil's wedding would have been. The dandelions were popping up everywhere, so I started picking a big bouquet. As I held the flowers in my little fist, I suddenly knew what to do.

Excitedly, I ran down the hill and pushed his door open without knocking. Theophil sat in his chair, and as I entered, he nodded at me in greeting. Determined, without a pause, I walked straight into the kitchen and grabbed a big spoon out of the drawer. Then I went straight to the letter, stood on tiptoes, and grabbed it off the mantel. I balled it up in my fist and pumped it in the air.

Theophil jumped out of his chair and croaked, "You leave that be. Put it back right now!"

I didn't. Instead, I ran out of the house with it. Theophil chased after me. Since he was weak and out of shape, my small body easily outran his long-legged stride. I ran straight up the hill and started digging a hole with the spoon in the shade of that cottonwood tree. By the time Theophil got there, the hole was big enough.

As he stood watching me with a stunned and confused expression, I put the letter in the hole and covered it with dirt. Then I took the bouquet of dandelions I had just picked and placed it on the mound. I turned around to see tears well up in Theophil's eyes. Though I hadn't realized it until then, I had been crying the whole time as well.

Side by side we sat on that hill, balling like a couple of babies. Then, as our tears dried, we just sat and watched the puffy white clouds move across the blue sky. It felt right. It felt comfortable. Eventually, Theophil turned to me and put an arm around my slim shoulders.

With a little hug, he finally spoke. "Thank you, Shadow. I think that's just what I needed. A funeral."

We sat together all afternoon and watched the sun go down. As its warmth fell behind the line of the horizon, the air became chilly. We didn't mind. In the peace of that evening, the fresh spring air revived Theophil with every breath. He was beginning to heal, and I had helped him. It was a good day.

After that, Theophil started farming again. I can't say he started living again, but he was at least trying. He continued to go through the motions, and each day he climbed further out of that dark place where he had been hiding for so long. It was good to have my friend back. Or at least coming back.

If you work hard and get your field and garden planted, you can take advantage of the lull in chores that comes in the late spring or early summer. That's just what Theophil did that year when he asked me if I wanted to go fishing.

As we walked to our fishing spot, Theophil told me he had started to remember how it felt to enjoy life. He remembered having hopes and dreams and taking pleasure in things. He said he used to love to fish. "I really can't say what I liked about it, but I sure as heck know I liked it!"

I felt the same. Even as an old lady, I love fishing as much as I did as a girl. I never even minded baiting my own hook or grabbing the slimy fish and putting it in the pail after I caught it.

While we were fishing, Theophil told me he had made a decision. Even though he still felt empty inside, he was going to start pretending he was happy. And remembering the ordinary things that used to bring him pleasure might remind him how to be happy again. We didn't catch anything that day, but sitting in the sunshine, listening to Theophil's voice, was wonderful.

A few weeks later, everyone stayed after church to celebrate the baptism of Hulda and Herman's first and only daughter, Regina. After three boys, Hulda was so happy to finally have a girl that she could hardly contain herself. Herman, for his part, couldn't stop smiling that morning as he watched Hulda dress Regina in the little pink and white batismal dress that was adorned in ribbons and lace. Regina was a beautiful, sweet baby, and the joy those parents felt for her was contagious. An energy of happiness that was almost palpable hung in the air.

Sometimes, when I'm feeling down, I close my eyes and think about that day. Remembering what happened always lifts my spirits.

Nowadays, the church is surrounded on three sides by the cemetery, but back then there were only three or four dozen graves on the east side. The green expanse on the south and west were adorned with just one or two trees, making it the perfect place for outdoor gatherings.

The families brought their most delicious home-cooked dishes to share for the occasion. There was so much to eat, it was hard to know where to begin. A few of the men rolled some stumps over and placed a couple of flat boards on them. That created the table for the food. Mrs. Sahli brought her German potato salad. She made it with onion, vinegar, salt, pepper, and just enough sugar to take the sting out. Mrs. Lindemann brought a big jar of her pickled beets. Herman and Hulda had supplied the stew with some of the meat from one of their freshly butchered cows.

As the afternoon turned to early evening, someone started playing the fiddle and a few couples started to dance. The music was lively, and the footwork and twirling of that polka was fast. The little boys ran around, pushing and wrestling each other to see who was the strongest. You know how boys are. The ladies sat together talking, laughing, and hollering at their little ones to behave. In other words, it was a near perfect day. The slanted rays of summer sun lit up that late afternoon, and there was hardly a breeze. Everyone was in a good mood.

Theophil stood with a few of the men who were talking about things men talk about. The best fishing spots, the best way to clear the rocks from the field, what to do with a sick animal. Theophil was distant, but he was listening and even took part in a bit of conversation.

Then, out of nowhere, little David came scampering by. David, one of Albert's boys, was about two years old. He wasn't looking where he was going. Maybe one of the other boys was chasing him, but knowing David, he might just have been running for no reason at all.

David ran right into his father's legs and caused him to lose his balance. Albert was holding a plate of food in one hand and lifting a glass of lemonade to his mouth in the other. His plate and everything on it went flying onto Theophil. Pickled beets and stew soaked the poor man's chest. At the same time, Albert started to choke a little on the lemonade. With a sudden cough, he spit the liquid out right into Theophil's face. He was a mess! The beets instantly stained his shirt purple, and thick, brown gravy dripped from his chest. He was covered in food and soaking wet with sticky lemonade. Though it happened in a flash, the result couldn't have been more thorough.

Everyone stopped. Frozen in their spots. Like they were all statues. I know I didn't breathe. We just didn't know what to do. No one was hurt, but we could hardly believe what just happened.

How could someone become such a mess so fast? And, most importantly, what would this do to poor Theophil? He was just coming back to us, and in that moment, I think we all were afraid the embarrassment would send him back to that dark place we'd worked so hard to bring him out of.

We were all staring at Theophil, and he was staring back at us. Then a big smile appeared, and not just on his mouth. That grin covered his whole face. Suddenly he was laughing! The chuckle shook his whole body. The kind of belly laugh you can only laugh when you're truly happy. Because he was laughing, everyone else started. We laughed until tears were coming out of our eyes and we had trouble breathing. We laughed until we forgot what we were laughing at, and then we laughed some more. Finally, Theophil was laughing so hard he fell to the ground and rolled around clutching his belly. That was the best sound I've ever heard.

That food mess was the best medicine in the world. Theophil told me later that once he started laughing, he couldn't stop. He felt like all the hurt and all the pain was being laughed right out of his body, and he never wanted it to find its way back. From that moment on, my friend was fully back. He became himself again.

We went fishing again some days later, and Theophil told me, "I'm not pretending anymore!" He was smiling when he said it. Truth is, he didn't have to say it. I could tell. He even seemed to walk taller and with more purpose. Boy, had I missed him!

That story of a lemonade-and-beet-juice-covered Theophil was told and retold for years after by almost everyone who was there. But the interesting thing is, if the person hearing it wasn't there, he'd make a slight grin or give the teller a little polite chuckle. In and of itself, it isn't really that humorous. But for those of us who were there, it has a power all its own. The same belly laughs start up again. In fact, sometimes people laugh even harder than they did that day.

What I'll never forget as long as I breathe is how that moment changed a man's life. It makes my heart sing just to think of it.

That's the funny thing about memories. They live inside us for as long as we let them. Memories are like a living thing. Remembering keeps them alive and maybe even causes them to grow. That's why I work hard to remember only the good times— to keep the happiness alive inside. When the bad times start to pop into my head, I try to replace them with something that will make me smile again. I can't do anything to change something bad that has passed, so why bring that misery into my present?

You may think my story of Theophil ends there, but it doesn't. A man like Theophil loves to be in love. He lamented, "I miss that unsettled feeling in my stomach I'd get when I looked at my ex- fiancée back home. I felt sick most of the time I was with her, but when I left her side, I just wanted that feeling again." He talked a lot about that feeling. He described it as a sort of hunger.

Theophil didn't really speak about his ex-fiancée back home specifically, and it didn't seem to me that he missed *her* that much. But he really missed that stomach ailment. I didn't understand it then, of course.

Theophil was still a storyteller, and he would often describe for me the times he spent with his ex-fiancée back home and her sister. The sister's name was Lydia, and Theophil's voice was always tender when he spoke it.

When I went over to his place after breakfast one day the next spring, he surprised me by saying, "I've been waitin' for you. I have somethin' to tell you. I wrote another letter to my ex-fiancée back home, and I want you to read it."

I could've fallen over. I thought for sure he was done with her. I didn't want to go through all that heartache with him or lose my friend again. What if he didn't come back a second time? I pushed the letter away, and tears instantly sprang to my eyes.

Theophil laughed at me. "Just read it," he urged. "It isn't what you think."

Boy, did he get that right. I couldn't have dreamed what I saw on that paper.

Dearest Emma,

It has taken me far too long to write you. Please accept my apology for my long silence. I was stunned by your response, and it has taken me a bit to accept it. I have been giving the matter a great deal of thought. I could never quite believe that our relationship was as one-sided as you indicated. I definitely felt my love returned. After many hours pondering our time together, I have come to realize that my love was returned. You see, I thought I was loving you this whole time. Now I understand that even though I was in your presence, the love I felt was from the other who was always with us. I have finally come to realize that I love and have always loved your sister, Lydia. And I hope she may have felt the same for me. I don't pretend to know what has happened in her life these many years. But if you find it in your heart, could you please ask Lydia to write to me? Tell her that my heart is hers for the taking, and if she will have this slow-witted man, he will spend a lifetime trying to bring happiness to her every breath!

I am ready, and I am waiting!

Theophil

"This man is daft!" I thought. A woman breaks his heart and nearly destroys him, and all of a sudden he wants the SISTER! I was quite angry with him. Why was he putting himself through this again? But what could I do? He wasn't asking me what I thought, and I wouldn't have been able to tell him if he did. I'm sure that's why he chose to read the letter to me. He knew anyone else would have thrown it in the fire and called him a lunatic. I guess that's my curse. I just listen. Nothing more.

A month went by. The leaves on the trees down by the lake had started to turn, and the big old cottonwood on the hill glowed yellow. The men were busy with the harvest, and the women were putting up produce and preparing for the winter ahead.

The winters are long, gray, and cold here. The snows are unpredictable. Heavy one year and almost non-existent the next. The only thing we can depend on is that the wind never stops howling. It whips right through the walls and pushes the cold into every pore of your body if you let it. People work hard to make sure they can survive whatever Mother Nature and this harsh climate can throw at them. Even in these modern times, folks still dig out their heaviest blankets and warm clothes in the fall so they're ready when the cold winds come again.

I saw a wagon pull up to Theophil's place. It wasn't so unusual. People loved Theophil and were always stopping by to hear a story if they were in the area. I'd just finished taking in the laundry and had a little time before I was to help with supper. I decided to run over and listen to Theophil's stories for a bit. So I was there to see the whole thing first hand.

As soon as the wagon stopped, or more accurately before it came to a complete stop, this incredibly beautiful woman jumped out and started running to the house calling out in a thick German accent, "Theophil! I'm here! I'm finally here!"

I had never laid eyes on this woman before, and I couldn't figure out who she was and what she wanted with Theophil. She sure was pretty, though. She had blonde, almost white, hair that bounced outside of her bun and bonnet in curly waves. Even from a distance, I could see her big blue eyes. They were so vivid, they almost looked like ice. But at the same time, they were the warmest, kindest eyes I've ever seen. I guessed she was a few years younger than Theophil—maybe about twenty-one. She was a little heavy, but I wouldn't say she was fat. She looked soft and curvy, like you just wanted to give her a hug or sit on her lap while she read you a story. Even though she was running around Theophil's yard like a headless chicken, I have to admit, I liked her from that first look.

Theophil wasn't in the house. He was at the far side of the barn chopping wood, so he didn't see or hear the commotion. I ran over to him, tapped his arm, and pointed at the stranger running all around his place.

Theophil dropped his axe, and his mouth hung open like his jaw wasn't attached. Finally, he shouted, "LYDIA?!!" And he set to running after her like a bull was chasing him. I never saw anything like it. They started hugging and kissing and crying all over each other.

The fellow that dropped Lydia off just looked at me, winked, set her bags down, and hopped back on the wagon. With a click, click to direct the horses, he was on his way.

I stood there for a few minutes but quickly realized those two didn't see anything but each other. The way they carried on, maybe they couldn't even see that much.

I went home and helped Hulda with supper. I kept my eye on Theophil's place, but Lydia didn't leave. In fact, she not only spent the night, but those two didn't leave that house for at least two full days!

As you'd expect, rumors were flying all over the village. It seemed this strange woman told the man at the station she was coming to "marry the love of her life." She and Theophil had known each other back in the old country and had loved each other since the beginning. That sparked plenty of conversation, speculation, and gossip. Everyone in the village knew about Theophil's ex-fiancée back home and that things had ended badly. No one could figure out what was going on, and some even thought Lydia might have meant him some harm. One neighbor suggested someone better check on him. Maybe Lydia had killed him in his sleep. I didn't really believe that, but after a couple days of not seeing either of them outside the house, I did get a little worried.

On the third day, Hulda said at breakfast, "Enough of this! I'm going over there!"

After we cleaned up from breakfast, she made her famous white frosted cake and headed for the door. Just as she was about to walk out, she called to me, "Shadow, you better come with. No telling what I might find, and I may need someone to run for help."

She didn't have to ask me twice. I was dying to get another look at Lydia, and I was as curious as could be. Even so, I wasn't prepared for what we'd find.

Hulda knocked on the door and called out, "Theophil, are you there?"

No sooner did she get the question out then the door swung open. Lydia had the biggest, friendliest smile on her face you ever saw. She said, "Come in, come in. Sit down and I'll get you a cup of coffee."

Lydia said this like it was her house. We were stunned by this greeting.

As we entered and our eyes adjusted to the dim light in the kitchen, we saw Theophil sitting at the table with a cup of coffee and the biggest smile I've ever seen on a man. He introduced Hulda. Then he stood, put his arm around me, and said, "Lydia, I want you to meet my special friend. She means the world to me, and I hope you'll like her half as much as I do. They call her Shadow."

I'd never been introduced as "special" before. I had no idea I meant so much to Theophil. Of course, he was my best friend, and I loved him with all my heart, but I really didn't know he felt the same for me. It caught me off guard, and tears came to my eyes.

Lydia jumped up and grabbed me. "Shadow! I'm so happy to meet you!" She gave me the biggest, warmest hug I ever received. "Theo has told me so much about you, I feel like I know you already. I hope we can be friends."

She noticed my tears and said, "Oh my! I'm so sorry. Did I hurt you? Sometimes I don't know what comes over me. I must have squeezed the very breath right out of you. Here, sit down, and I'll get you some water."

Needless to say, in that instant I loved Lydia as much as I ever loved Theophil. It tickled me that she called him *Theo*. I'd never heard anyone call him that, but it suited him. It made me almost forget she was a stranger who didn't belong in his house. But as I looked around, it seemed as if the house had been waiting for her. Though it wasn't exactly different, it sure wasn't the same. The furniture had been rearranged a bit, some new pictures sat on the mantel, and a couple of new quilts hung over the backs of the chairs. I noticed some lace doilies and a few other womanly touches. The place had never looked better.

Hulda got straight to it. She set down her cake, took a sip of her coffee, and started battering them both with questions. We soon discovered that Lydia was the sister of the woman who broke Theophil's heart. Lydia knew all about his love for her sister and didn't care a bit. She said she always knew that her Theo would come to discover his true heart. She never doubted him for a moment.

Then Hulda laid into them. She told them their behavior was improper and that people had already started to talk. It wasn't right that two unmarried young people should be hugging and kissing each other in the yard, much less spending the night together without a chaperone. As they sat with ashamed and red cheeked faces, Hulda kept preaching, making it sound as if they were headed straight to hell. As if the good Lord Himself would surely appear on the doorstep any moment and strike us all down in an instant.

As embarrassed as they looked, Lydia and Theophil took the scolding well enough, sneaking little grins at each other throughout the whole ordeal. They explained they planned to get married that Sunday after service if the preacher had time.

Hulda thought it would be best for Lydia to stay at her place until they were married, but there was no way Theophil was going to let Lydia out of his sight. Hulda must have realized this, too. I was surprised she didn't dig her feet in more than she did. Usually once Hulda had her mind set on a thing, that thing happened one way or another. As a compromise, Hulda finally said, "Well, have it your way. You have to live with yourselves. But, I think it would be best if Shadow stayed. That should keep things from getting further outta hand than they already are."

Hulda stayed a of couple hours, and all that time Lydia chattered ecstatically about how excited she was to meet the neighbors and begin her new life with her *Theo*.

The next few nights, I slept at Theophil's place. I liked the warm comfort of his house, and I loved listening to them coo at each other. Theophil couldn't keep his eyes off her. Lydia seemed completely at home. She was a good cook, too. That first night she made stewed chicken with dumplings and apple pie for dessert. I showed her where the tree was and helped her pick and peel enough apples for that pie. She treated me kindly, as if she truly enjoyed having me around.

Hulda spread the word quickly. A steady stream of visitors called at Lydia and Theophil's house, and that Sunday the church was standing room only. The preacher didn't have a choice whether to marry them or not. The town would have lynched him if he said no.

Over the months ahead, Lydia and I became close. I spent even more time at Theophil's place than I had before. Lydia gave birth to her first baby within the year. Everyone was so happy for them, but no one more than me. Theophil, Lydia, and now little Harry.

Just so I can move on to something else, I'll tell you how their story ends. Lydia and Theophil had fourteen children. One died a few days after birth, and another got sick and died before her third birthday. But twelve survived, and their parents loved each one as much as the first.

Their grandson, Elmer, now works the farm with his wife and young son. Elmer stops by to visit every couple weeks, and I sometimes spend holidays with their family. He resembles Theophil in both his appearance and in his loving heart. Elmer likes to tell stories, too, and even has some of the same speech patterns. Last week, he stopped by, and when I opened the door, he said, "Hello, Shadow. Looks like we're gonna get some rain, not?"

As I write their story, I'm happy that Lydia's sister Emma was so cold-hearted. If Theophil hadn't gone through that pain, I don't think he could ever have fully rejoiced in his happiness and love for Lydia. Like any married couple, those two fought over the years, and with all those kids, they struggled for sure. But their love was pure and strong. It's difficult now to think about them separately. They belonged together. It just took a little time and a lot of pain before they realized it.

Nicklaus

Most of my life has been spent watching others live out their lives. Or listening to people tell their stories. This suits me. But as painful as it will be, I feel compelled to write one story—a love story—that is mine and mine alone. Yes, even I have a love story.

When you look at this old, wrinkled face, it may be difficult to see the young girl I once was. But I can assure you, she is inside this withering body. As much as I want to share my story, I've been procrastinating the last few days. It will bring back many feelings and memories, making them seem all too real again. I guess that's the whole point, though. These events happened, and the good Lord continues to nag me to get them down on paper. So enough with the delay. Let me start. I only hope I can bring it to life for you so you will understand.

I was about seventeen years old. Of course, since I've never celebrated a birthday, there's no way to say for sure how old I was. The point is, I was a girl on the verge of becoming a woman. I was interested in the village boys and even looked their way a few times, if you know what I mean. Many of my friends spoke of being sweet on this boy or that one. I'd heard many stories from the older folks about love and flirtations as I sat quietly in the corner, unnoticed. And I'd witnessed Theophil and Lydia's love blossom right in front of me. Still, I understood that people like me didn't get to fall in love. I was too different. I just sat on the outside looking in.

That's why I was caught so off guard. You see, it was an ordinary fall day. The air was crisp and clean. Not heavy with the humid air that often oppresses the summer afternoons. The skies were bright blue, and there wasn't a hint of the cold, bitter winds that winter would soon bring our way.

As I've said, Lydia and I became close friends over the years. She needed help with all those little ones, and I looked for every excuse to spend time at their place because I always felt so warm and comfortable there. That day, Lydia was getting low on a few things she needed for the next morning's baking. She asked if I'd mind walking the three miles to town to get her some flour and sugar. I was happy to help out and even happier for an excuse to get out in the fresh air. So off I went. Just like a hundred times before.

It had rained off and on a few days before, so even though the sky was bright, there were mud puddles all over the road. I tried to walk in the ditch to avoid the muck, but the high grass there held all the moisture from the recent rains. It took me longer than usual to get to town, and by the time I arrived, my shoes and socks were wet clean through to my toes. The hem of my skirt had taken on the water like a sponge, and the bottom of my dress clung to my legs. I must have looked a fright, but I never worried much about that. Most people didn't really notice me, anyway.

As I arrived in town, I decided to sit for a bit on the little bench in front of the post office. I wanted to soak in as much of that sunshine as I could before the sky turned gray again. It was also a good place to dry off.

As I sat there, I saw an unfamiliar and handsome boy—or more accurately, young man—walk down the middle of the road. He held himself straight and tall with his strong shoulders pulled back like he was proud. I'd never seen him before. He looked about my age or maybe a few years older. His hair was blond. Not white like some you see, and not yellow like others. It was more like the color of sand. He was tall, too—over six foot if he was an inch. He had on a dark blue shirt and some worn-out overalls that were a little short for his long legs. I couldn't take my eyes off him.

As he walked past, he turned and looked at me sitting on that bench. He took one step more and then stopped and looked again. I swear, such a feeling came over me that I thought I was having some sort of attack. My stomach started to do this funny flipping thing, and I had trouble swallowing. I felt as though I had a fever because my face became so hot. I decided I should get up and go straight to Doc's office. An illness that comes on that suddenly couldn't be good.

As I stood, this young man walked in my direction. As he came closer, I realized that he wasn't planning to go into the post office as I first thought. Instead, he was coming to talk to me. I had to sit back down. Whatever had overtaken me made my knees buckle, and I thought I was going to tip over right there on Main Street.

He was chewing on a blade of grass and smiled as he approached. The blade was stuck in one of his back teeth. His deep blue eyes sparkled as he approached. This fever I had caught must be going around because his cheeks were all red and flushed just like mine felt. I hoped we weren't on the verge of some sort of epidemic.

The young man approached and said, "Hello there. My name's Nicklaus. I'm new to these parts. I'm staying over at the Schmidt farm until I can get myself set up. Kasper Schmidt is my father's cousin, and he's helping me. What's your name?"

I felt panicked. I wanted to tell him my name, but I don't even know what my name is. Just as I was wondering how I was going to get away and find the doctor, a twelve-year-old, David, approached. Until that moment, I didn't even realize there was another soul in town. I have no idea where he came from or how long he'd been standing there. But, there he was, right by my side.

David stood tall and puffed out his boyish chest. Making his voice sound deeper than it was, he said, "Her name's Shadow.

She don't talk. She lives over the hill at Herman's place. Shadow doesn't talk, but she listens real good. She's one of the nicest people I know, so you better not be thinking anything!"

What an odd thing for David to say, I thought. It was the strangest day! David appeared out of nowhere and said such nice things about me. Then he seemed ready to defend me from this good-looking stranger. I didn't even realize David thought about me, much less that he thought I was nice or a good listener. He was such a sweet little thing.

Nicklaus looked at me, "Is that true, Shadow? You don't talk?"

I nodded, and then I could swear he winked at me. It was a quick little eye twitch, so I couldn't be certain, but it sure seemed like he did it on purpose.

Nicklaus smiled at David and said, "Pleased to make your acquaintance. I didn't catch your name."

"David."

"Do you play baseball, David?"

David nodded. "I'm probably the best pitcher around, too!"

Nicklaus said, "Well I could've guessed that by looking at those strong arms of yours. I bet you're fast, too. How long do you think it would take you to run to that white house at the far end of town and back, do you think?"

David said, "You mean Mrs. Deis's house? That's probably a half mile from here. That's a long way, but I'm fast."

Nicklaus said, "Why don't we see? I'll wait right here with Shadow, and we'll count the seconds until you get back."

Before David could respond, Nicklaus counted, "One, two, three" and then shouted, "GO!" at the top of his lungs.

Poor David was so stunned and confused, he looked like he didn't know what else to do but take off running.

As soon as David was gone, Nicklaus looked at me again and smiled a little half smile. He said, "I figure we'll get about ten minutes before he gets back and tries to fight me for you." Then he winked at me again. This time, I was sure of it.

Really, I was overcome. Nicklaus didn't look at me as if I was strange. He looked at me like I was a person. He winked at me like he was flirting. I don't remember standing up, but I had to sit back down because my legs had turned to water. As I sat down, this young man sat down next to me! It was almost more than I could bear.

He looked at me as his head moved close to mine and gave a little nod. "So, you really don't talk, huh? Not even a word or two?"

I shook my head.

"Hmmm. I ain't never met anyone that didn't talk before." He paused a moment in reflection. "I bet it's kinda peaceful. I bet it gives you more time to hear things, huh?"

No one had ever talked to me like this before. Even Lydia didn't ask me questions about myself. I shrugged my shoulders in response to Nicklaus's question. I hoped he would ask me more. And he did.

"Is your name really Shadow?"

I shrugged. As you know, I really don't know what my name is, but Shadow is what people call me and it's the name I answer to, so maybe that makes it mine.

"That's a funny name. Do you like it?"

Truthfully, I hadn't really given it any thought. I shrugged my shoulders again and wrinkled my nose a little so he would know that I didn't much care for it but it didn't bother me, either.

Nicklaus said, "I don't think that name suits you. A Shadow is dark and follows behind a person. Someone as pretty as you should have a name that describes how a person feels when he sees you. How about….let me think…how 'bout I call you Ray? You know, like a ray of sunshine. Sunrays are bright and beautiful and always make people feel warm and happy. Can I call you Ray?"

I couldn't believe what I was hearing. The handsome young man with the smooth low voice and blade of grass hanging in the corner of his full lipped mouth just said I was pretty! No boy had ever even looked at me before. Now this one just said I was pretty. Something must be wrong with him because, if you remember, I was a bit of a mess with my wet and muddy shoes and my skirt still clinging to my legs from the damp grass.

I nodded a little to let him know I liked being called Ray. Now my face really got hot, and it dawned on me that somehow Nicklaus was causing this fever.

All of a sudden I heard David's voice beside me. He was panting heavily and had a big grin on his face. "Well, I'm fast, ain't I?"

Nicklaus sighed, "Maybe too fast, boy, maybe too fast. Any chance I can talk you into trying to beat your time?"

"Nope, not today. I got to get back and start my chores. Shadow, you coming? I'll walk ya." Then turning to Nicklaus, he said, "See ya 'round, I guess."

With that we headed back. I felt a little dizzy. Even though David had bragged about me being a good listener, I can tell you, I only heard a few of the words he said on that walk home. From what I gathered, though, he was chattering away about how fast and strong he was and how he hoped that new fella would be around for a while.

David liked Nicklaus. I did, too. Even if he did make me feel ill.

We were about a mile down the road before I remembered that the reason I went to town was to get some supplies for Lydia. Oh my! That wasn't like me at all. What could I do? I motioned to David that I was heading back to town and he should go on without me. He frowned a little but continued on down the road.

I ran back to town, all the while hoping to see and hoping not to see Nicklaus. I longed to hear his voice, but I was just starting to feel like myself, and I was scared of that sickness coming over me again. Fortunately or unfortunately, I didn't see him. I picked up the flour and sugar and started back home for the second time that day. What a day!

As I walked back, I couldn't stop going over that conversation with Nicklaus in my mind again and again.

He winked at me! He said I was pretty! Was he teasing me? It didn't feel like he was, and there was no one around but David to show off to. And he sent David off for a run and didn't even pretend to watch him. Could he truly have been flirting with me? No. People like me don't get flirted with. Tall, handsome, young men who could get the attention of any girl in town—they especially do not flirt with people like me.

I sighed as I made my way back, thinking, "This will be a day to remember, but that's all it will ever amount to."

When I arrived at Theophil's place, the afternoon sun had almost disappeared below the horizon. The sky was a brilliant reddish orange, which meant the wind would blow strong the next day. Lydia was at the cook stove starting supper. Theophil was just coming in from the field to clean up, and the little ones were about the house as usual. Things were as normal as could be. Nothing changed. How odd, when for me, everything had changed.

The next day I was sitting on the front porch. A few years before, Hulda had told Herman she needed a proper porch to sit on in the heat of the day. Herman and their boys set out building a porch and then even made a few rocking chairs, a bench, and a two-person swing to put out there. I was happy Hulda had insisted on it. The family and I spent many a day and evening on that porch. It was pleasant back then, and it still is. Last Easter, the boys invited me over after church. We sat on that very porch drinking coffee after dinner.

As I said, I was sitting on the front porch churning some butter for the week ahead. The late morning was a little cooler than the day before, but the sky was just as blue and, as predicted, the wind was strong. Fortunately, the house blocked the breeze, so I was quite comfortable with just a sweater to warm my shoulders. It was the kind of day made for counting your blessings, and that's just what I was doing. I had so much to be thankful for: a place to sleep, food to eat, and people around me I cared about. Hulda had opened the big wood door so the heat of the kitchen could escape through the screen door. Even though I could hear everything going on in the house, I wasn't really paying attention.

As I sat there looking out at the horizon, a man on a horse appeared in the distance. As he drew near, I couldn't believe my eyes. It was Nicklaus! What in the world could he be doing here? I wondered. My stomach started doing those flips again, and I ran into the house, letting the door slam shut behind me. I wanted to find a good spot where I could go unnoticed but still hear what he wanted.

Hulda was in the kitchen baking bread. "What has gotten into you today, Shadow? Are you sick? You've been acting strange ever since you got back from Theophil's place yesterday. I declare, if you think you're gonna get out of your chores 'cause you're a little outta sorts, you have another think comin'! Winter's gonna be here soon, and there's a heap of work to be done…."

As Hulda was scolding me, I found the little stool that I kept in the shadow of the kitchen on the far side of the fire. I sat down and looked at the floor, trying to make myself as small as I could. Then there was a little knock at the door, and Nicklaus's face appeared on the other side of the screen.

"Good day, ma'am. My name's Nicklaus Haberer. I just arrived by train a week ago, and I'm staying over at the Schmidt place. Kasper Schmidt is my father's cousin, and he said he'd put me up 'til I could settle into my own place."

Nicklaus looked dressed for church. He had on a nice, clean red shirt that looked freshly pressed. He wore black pants and matching suspenders. His sandy hair was slicked down with oil. Even from a few feet away, I could smell the fresh scent of soap on him. Oh, I hoped I didn't get sick right there in my little chair. He was casting some sort of magic spell on me to make me sick—and somehow, I liked it.

I finally understood what Theophil was talking about all those years earlier when he described how he felt with his fiancée back home. Now I had some sort of stomach ailment, and I just wanted more.

Hulda smiled broadly. "Well, do come in and sit a spell. It's good to see a strong young man come to settle in these parts. We could do with a new face 'round here. I 'spose you come to talk with Herman? He's out on the other side of the hill bringin' in the last of the potatoes. If you hold on a minute, I'll get little Regina to fetch him."

"Ah, well, no ma'am. I actually came to call on Ray, I mean, Shadow."

His eyes scanned the house, and I felt the heat of them when they landed on me. His face turned a little red when he saw me. He looked nervous.

"What?" Hulda stared at me, then him. "What do you want with Shadow? How do you even know her?"

"I met her in town yesterday in front of the post office. We talked a spell." When Hulda's eyes narrowed with suspicion, he added, "Well, I guess I did the talkin'."

She put her hands on her hips. "Are you trying to be smart or something? I don't take kindly to people coming around here trying to cause trouble."

Nicklaus looked pained. "I promise you, ma'am, I'm not trying to cause any trouble. I just wanted to sit a spell on that nice porch of yours with Shadow."

Hulda looked him over good. She took a long time with her response. As she thought it over, I sat on my little stool bewildered. What could he want with me? I hadn't stopped thinking about him, but I was surprised he even remembered me. Was he really calling on me?

As Hulda took her time deciding whether she would allow him to sit with me, I looked over at Nicklaus. When our eyes met, he threw another of those winks my way. I nearly fell right off that little stool!

Hulda finally sighed deeply. "Well, go on then. I don't imagine you could get into too much mischief with me on the other side of the door. Keep in mind, I'm right here, and I can hear everythin' you're sayin' and see everythin' you're doin'!"

Nicklaus looked over at me and smiled, "How 'bout it, Ray?"

I couldn't help but smile back. I left that little dark spot by the fire and followed the strange, sandy-haired creature out to the porch. I sat in the chair, and Nicklaus took a seat on the bench. He didn't say much. He mostly just looked at me and grinned. But he whispered something to me I'll never forget.

"Ray, I can't stop thinking about you. You're so pretty, you stopped me in my tracks yesterday!"

Even if I did talk, I couldn't have put a complete thought together. I was sitting out on the front porch with a gentleman caller. Me!

The whole time I knew Nicklaus, we didn't have any trouble communicating. He seemed to be able to read my thoughts by the expressions on my face. I would nod, shrug, point, laugh, and frown. Nicklaus often did the same, and even on that first day, we seemed to have a silent language only the two of us understood.

Nicklaus left after a half hour or so. I waved good-bye to him, and then sat down to finish churning the butter. The rest of the night, the whole house was buzzing about my visitor. The little ones looked at me and giggled while Hulda re-told the story to Herman about five times. I listened and wanted to hear it all again and again. It made everything seem more real. Herman just shook his head and kept repeating, "I don't know what to make of it."

That crisp fall day was the start of my romance.

Hulda knew how to get information, and that's just what she did. She told me a few days later that this boy was nothing but trouble. Hulda warned that he boarded the boat for America because he'd no other choice. It was either leave for America or spend the rest of his days in jail or worse. Apparently, Nicklaus had a bad temper and burned down the family church. She warned me to stay clear of him. She said it as if her declaration made it final. I was to stay away. It had been decided.

I couldn't believe what she told me. When I looked into his eyes, I felt I could see his soul. I have a knack for seeing people for who they really are. I learn a lot from the way a person holds his head, how his eyes move, and the way he sits when he talks. Mostly, I just get a feeling. And I felt strongly that this stranger was a very good person.

Nicklaus pursued me. That's really the only way to say it. He saw me whenever he could. We met at church on Sundays, of course, but sometimes, we planned to see each other elsewhere, too. He always made sure to tell me if he was going to be in town or if he thought he might take an afternoon to go fishing. I did my best to break away and find him every chance I got.

It was the first and possibly the only time I ever disobeyed Hulda. I did feel bad for the betrayal, but not bad enough to stay away from my sweet Nicklaus. You see, that's how I came to think of him: as mine.

Oh, the memory of those first few weeks with Nicklaus warms me. How I long to bring those fleeting moments back. I think I'll stop writing for tonight so I can savor the innocence of it all a little while longer. Because I know how this story ends, and I'm in no rush to get there.

That winter came early. The first snowfall happened in mid-October. It wasn't particularly cold, and the wind didn't blow most days. But the snow fell regularly. We'd get a few inches, then it would turn a little colder, and a few days later it would warm a bit and snow again. The cycle went on like that until the end of February. The snowbanks were halfway up the side of the barn by the time the weather warmed enough to start melting them. Eventually, though, the snows always turn to rain, and so the time goes on.

That long winter, Nicklaus and I didn't see much of each other except at church on Sundays. He started to walk me home when the weather permitted. Eventually, the townsfolk and even Hulda started to warm to him. He was charming and had an easy quality that most couldn't resist. Nicklaus would come in and sit a spell when Hulda or Herman invited him, which they usually did. I didn't know one person who met Nicklaus who didn't seem to like him. He didn't talk too much like some people do, yet he always kept up his end of the conversation. He was really clever but never made anyone he talked to feel less clever himself.

Nicklaus was hardworking, too. Hard work was always admired in those days. He started cutting the sod to make his house that fall and had it almost finished by the time the snows got heavy. We walked over to his place one day, and he showed me where he would plant his garden and where he would build the barn. He had a spot picked out for the cows, pigs, and chickens he wanted to have. The way he described his place, I could almost see it. The best part was that he always made it sound as if I was going to be a part of it all.

One day, as I was on my way to town delivering a basket of food to a friend of Regina's who had fallen ill, we crossed paths just as a blustery wind started to whip all that snow around. We weren't really prepared for a storm that day. But when that wind started to whip around, we could barely see.

Out here on the prairie, it doesn't take much of a breeze to kick up the snow and blow it around. Even nowadays there aren't many trees to block the wind, but there were even fewer back then. Nicklaus and I managed to make our way to the little sod house near the side of the road where Oskar and his young family used to live. Oskar had abandoned his place and left the area the previous year after his oldest son was kicked in the chest by a mule and died.

Anyway, Nicklaus and I were happy to find our way out of the blizzard. The door was unlocked, and there was even a little firewood left. Nicklaus didn't waste any time building a fire, and soon we were safe and warm.

That day as we sat side by side, Nicklaus told me about his childhood and how excited he'd been to get to America. He told me about all his hopes and dreams and how happy he'd been to find me. Eventually he told me about the night when the church burned down. He and his younger brother, Kermit, who was fourteen years old at the time, stayed after service one Sunday to chop wood for the stove. There never seemed to be enough from one week to the next. Nicklaus shared with his brother the secret he had been keeping from his family for more than six months. He was leaving for America the next day. He knew that his loved ones would try to talk him out of the plan so he made his preparations without anyone knowing. He would tell them all in the morning, kiss his mother and board the ship for the New World. Kermit became angry. He didn't want Nicklaus to go.

Nicklaus explained that it was time for him to make his own way in life and that America held the promise of prosperity and freedom. He told Kermit that he could join him in a few years when he was older. The conversation didn't go well. His brother accused him of abandoning the family. He said that he didn't care about any of them and he wouldn't be missed. When he thought back on it, Nicklaus realized Kermit didn't mean to hurt him. He just didn't want his brother to leave him behind. Nicklaus tried to calm him, but the conversation quickly turned into a loud argument.

As the argument escalated, Nicklaus's brother grabbed a piece of kindling and held it in the fire. He said he was going to burn the wood pile so Nicklaus would have to stay to chop more. Before Nicklaus could stop him, Kermit threw the lit piece of wood into the driest part of the pile. It burst into flames as soon as it landed. They were both stunned. Kermit hadn't intended to start the whole church on fire. He was just trying to get Nicklaus's attention. Nicklaus said his brother was known for his temper and occasional bad moods, but deep down, he was a good boy. He would never do something so horrible on purpose. At least that's what Nicklaus hoped.

The two boys looked around for something to put the flames out, but there was nothing at hand. The fire grew and overwhelmed the little church with its intense heat.

Nicklaus and his brother ran outside and right into a small group of villagers. When the shopkeeper asked what had happened, Nicklaus looked at the flaming church and then back at his brother. He swallowed and said, "It was me, sir. I wanted to leave something for people to remember me by."

Nicklaus took a quick look at his brother and saw the tears stream down his cheeks. Nicklaus ran and hid in the woods until the next morning. He walked aboard that ship without saying a proper good-bye to his parents or his grandparents. It was hard for him to recall this story, but I think it helped him to talk about it. He'd never told anyone the truth. He said he preferred to have people think badly of him rather than expose his brother.

As the wind continued to whip around outside, Nicklaus continued to tell me about his life. Despite the storm, it was a good day. That was the day he told me he loved me for the first time. He said it like I already knew it. He said, "I just love you so much, Ray, and I can't wait until the day I can make you mine."

He loved me! I can't describe to you what that felt like. My heart pounded with the realization. He LOVED me! How could anyone ever feel the happiness that I felt at that moment? HE loved me! He loved ME!

It was in that moment that I truly came to understand the power of words. Even though I didn't use them myself, I felt their strength and might. On that day, I experienced how words can change the course of a person's life. Good or bad words are a powerful tool. But, without words, I could only smile.

As the wind died down that evening and we made our way home, I realized that for the first time, I wanted to talk. I knew I could talk but chose not to. I can't say why exactly except that I've never liked the way the words tasted in my mouth. I didn't talk as a child, and as I grew older, I realized the beauty that rests in silence. I just liked it better that way.

Over the years I'd halfheartedly tried to talk once or twice. I croaked out some sounds on occasion, and it wasn't completely out of the ordinary for me to hum a little when I was alone. But, in that moment, something inside me changed. I didn't want to be different anymore. And I desperately wanted to tell Nicklaus that I loved him, too.

After that day, I snuck off to the barn, and when I was sure I was alone, I practiced talking to the cows and chickens. I sounded awful at first. My throat ached and felt tight and scratchy. I even cried the first few times because of the discomfort. I wanted to tell Nicklaus how much he meant to me and how proud I was to be his sweetheart. I needed him to know that I wanted to pass the rest of my days by his side. But how could I profess any of these feelings with such a vulgar sounding voice?

I was determined, though, and after several months, I felt my voice was ready to be heard. But I wanted to wait until just the right moment. I needed these first words to be special.

***

As the winter turned to spring, folks were anxious to get outside. It felt good to be able to deeply breathe the fresh air into our lungs. The long, cold winter and the threat of the Blue Death that plagued the area that season had left us all with a bad case of cabin fever. On a particularly warm Sunday in late April, Herbert Baum invited the entire congregation over to his place for a picnic. His property bordered a sizable lake with a nice sandy area for sunbathing in the summer. The ice had just completely melted a few weeks before, and the water was still very cold. When the snow melted, it caused quite a bit of flooding in the area. That spring, the shore was muddy rather than sandy, which made it difficult to walk without falling. In fact, several of the party goers did stumble and fall in the mud. It made both young and old laugh and added to the overall enjoyment of the outing.

This particular spot of the lake is unusual because it's very shallow for the first several yards and then has some steep drop-offs where the earth below gives way and seems to open up. It's a great spot to fish because you can wade out into the water up to your waist and then cast your line into the deeper waters where the big perch like to hide. This fishing spot is well known in these parts for that reason.

With so many covered in mud and it being such an unexpectedly warm day, several decided to walk out into the water to splash around and clean up a bit. Even with the flooding, you could walk out several feet without any fear of the drop off. Herbert kept yelling at people to stay back, but no one paid him much mind.

Nicklaus and I were sitting in the grass under a tree, and Nicklaus was chatting and laughing with the others. I had secretly decided that this was the perfect day for me to speak my words of love to him. I was waiting for just the right time, when we would be alone and no one would overhear.

As I waited for my opportunity, Edith Schoenmann yelled out for help. We all looked up, and she said with a toothless look of embarrassment, "I lost my false teeth! Please, someone help me find them!"

It seemed as if the whole party, young and old alike, went into the water to help her find those teeth. It was fun watching everyone dive in the waist deep, murky water feeling around for those dentures. Several people pulled up stones and sticks, thinking they had found the object of everyone's interest. It was like a grown-up game of hide and seek.

Nicklaus winked at me. "How 'bout it, Ray? Want to join them?"

I shook my head no. I knew this was the opportunity I was waiting for. Nicklaus and I were alone under that tree. He was laughing, and when he turned to look at me, I swallowed hard. I said, "I love you, too, Nicklaus."

To my great surprise, my voice sounded clearer and stronger than it ever had in the barn. It cracked a little as I said his name, but I believe that was caused by the emotions that welled up inside me.

Tears sprang to his eyes and to mine, too. He was so overcome it took him a while to say anything. When he finally did speak, he said, "Hearing you say my name with those words is a more beautiful song than any bird has ever sung! Ray, will you marry me? Please, say yes and marry me before planting season. I can't wait another season to have you all to myself!"

I was crying full out now and felt more happiness and joy than I've ever felt before or since. I said, "Of course, I will marry you, my love!"

He put his arm around my shoulders and gave me a kiss on my wet and teary cheek. Then, he licked his lips and said, "You taste salty."

We laughed and laughed.

As we reveled in our joy, the screams and shouts of laughter and fun from the lake changed to screams and shouts of horror and then to cries for help. There was true terror in the voices of our friends and neighbors. We looked up to see that Edith was gone as others fell below the surface of the water, too.

You see, in those days, hardly anyone knew how to swim. There weren't many lakes around, and there wasn't a lot of time for playing in the water. People spent time fishing and splashing around a little, but learning to swim was never a priority.

It seems that the crowd of merry makers waded out just a little too far and accidentally pushed Edith into the drop off. As she went under the water, her husband grabbed her, and she pulled him under as well. As people in the group tried to save each other, one by one they also fell victim to the drop-off. The water was frigid. Muscles stiffened and seized quickly. I'll never forget the horrible sounds of those screams as people splashed frantically in the water.

Nicklaus turned to me and said, "Ray, I can swim. I have to go." He wasn't asking for permission but was stating a fact.

My mouth went dry. I croaked, "Please, no."

He looked at me through his moistening eyes and said, "Don't you see, I have no choice. They're dying."

I looked at the water and knew he was right. As he turned and ran toward the water, I yelled, "Don't leave me!" I have no way of knowing if he heard me or not.

***

Nicklaus ran to the water and swam straight to the drop off. He pulled someone up out of the depths and dragged him to shore. He turned and swam out again. Soon, sweet young David was helping him. Without speaking, they seemed to have an understanding of each other's role in the rescue.

Nicklaus would drag the person half way and throw him or her at David. David would take the victim the rest of the way and go out for another. The problem was that as one would recover on shore, he would head straight out to the murderous waters again. As quickly as Nicklaus and David saved one, another would jump back in.

Those drowning were only an arm's length away from those standing in waist deep water. It should be so easy to save them. Just take one step closer and reach out a hand. But that one step put the rescuer in the drop off and turned him into another victim.

I could understand the irresistible temptation to save the drowning. Even now, as I remember the scene, it's hard to comprehend the horror. Because of the drop off, a man standing in the waist-deep water would watch as, just a yard beyond his reach, his wife or child disappeared under the surface. To be that close and be unable to save a loved one was more than many could resist. They couldn't stop themselves from going one step too far.

People were screaming for help as they splashed around in the icy waters trying to keep their heads above the surface. Others were shouting for those on shore to stay on land so they wouldn't fall victim themselves.

Soon, David gave up on the dragging to shore and started pushing and punching people as they tried to re-entered the water. He did everything his small thirteen-year-old body could to keep people from wading back in and sinking straight to their own deaths.

I was on the shore trying to tend to people as best as I could. I found if I turned them on their sides and pounded on their backs, they sometimes started coughing and then breathing again.

The tragic ordeal seemed to go on for hours. Everything was happening in slow motion. In reality, it couldn't have taken more than half an hour before it was all over.

In the end, three women, two men, and a young child lay dead on that beach. The sobs and cries went from ear-shatteringly loud to soft, steady, heaving breaths.

After a time I turned to find Nicklaus. I didn't see him. I got up and started running up and down the muddy beach. Where was he? Where could he have gone?

Suddenly, I heard a man's voice say, "Dear God in Heaven!" I turned to look at the water and saw two bodies floating to the surface. David went out and retrieved the entangled bodies. As he brought them to dry land, it looked as though Mrs. Deis had somehow climbed on top of Nicklaus. His face and arms were covered in bloody scratches and bruises. Mrs. Deis's face was frozen in horror, a silent scream still visible on her open mouth. We believe that as Nicklaus attempted to save her, she wrapped her arms around his head and neck in fear and took them both below the surface where they met their untimely deaths.

Two days later they found the body of little Ruby Schmidt, age three, about fifty yards down from the picnic area. No one knows how she drowned that day.

I don't remember seeing the lilacs in bloom that year. Hulda had planted lilacs on the property before the house was even finished. I used to count the days each year until that annual floral explosion. I still do. Such big purple blossoms, so fragrant you can almost taste them in the air. Each year, I mourn their passing when they fade away. But that year, the lilacs came and went unnoticed. I mourned a far greater loss.

It's been several days since I've written anything more. I've had to force myself to sit back down to finish this story. While it doesn't have a happy ending, there is a sweetness to it that I want to share with you before I'm done with it.

As you can imagine, this was a very dark time in our community. The big city newspaper even sent a reporter out here to the prairie to interview those who witnessed the tragic events of that day. Most folks didn't want to or simply couldn't talk about it. But others couldn't stop talking about it. People deal with things in different ways. There is no right or wrong in it; there's just coping.

Writing this down so many years later and thinking about how I can finish this tale has caused me to relive the ordeal. The removal of the bodies from the lakeshore, the planning of the funerals, the burials, the intimate conversations, and most of all the sobbing. There's nothing to be gained from retelling those tales. And, truthfully, I couldn't bear the pain of putting it all in writing.

I decided to walk by the shore where it all happened. I hoped it might help me put the right ending on this story. It was a beautiful walk, and I'm glad I decided to visit the spot one last time. Now that I'm older, the walk is difficult, so I don't think I'll ever venture out that way again.

The beach is gone now, taken over by grassland. The Baum family sold the property a year or so later, and a nice young couple settled there. They were respectful of both the dead and the living. They allowed all who wished to visit the site to do so whenever and however often they chose. Their grandson now runs the farm and has done a fine job keeping up the fields. He knows the story and has paid careful attention to tending the trees.

The trees. I was stunned by their size. You see, Hulda, who was not even there that day, decided something had to be done to mark the spot. She remembered seeing some sad-looking trees from the train window as we made our way from the East to the prairie. She remarked to no one in particular that these trees looked hunched over as if they carried a heavy burden. A gentleman in a seat across the aisle told her they were called "weeping willow trees" for that very reason.

After the tragedy, Hulda sent away for some saplings of those sad trees. She planted nine trees that year, one for each of the lives that was lost. Hulda nurtured and cared for them as if they were her own children until the day she died.

Hulda could be a hard, stubborn woman, but the gesture of caring for those trees should show you the loving character that hid beneath her crusty exterior. As I sat under the shade of those tall, beautifully sad trees the other day, my heart swelled with love for that woman, long gone now, who could have left me without a second thought on that ship but instead accepted me as her burden and took me in.

As I sat by the lake under those weeping branches, I realized there's something else that I need to tell you before I move on to happier times.

After my Nicklaus died, I spent much of my time alone, walking. I just walked here and there with no real direction or purpose. I felt that if I kept myself moving, I could somehow find a place where I didn't feel so much loss.

One day, as I walked down our little main street and was just about out of town, David came up beside me. Sweet David, still a boy but growing into a man. He confessed to me that he felt he should have done more. He said he thought if he had acted sooner or moved faster, he could have saved more lives. I was in such pain I hadn't taken the time to think how others might be feeling.

I stopped and turned to him. I grabbed him by the shoulders and hugged him. We stood in this embrace for a time, and then I saw a large rock by the side of the road. I motioned, and we walked over to sit down. I sat on the rock, and David on the ground.

He was quiet for a long time. Then he looked at his feet and whispered, "I heard you, Shadow. I heard you that day with Nicklaus. I know you can talk."

I was shocked and embarrassed. In truth, I'd almost forgotten that I spoke. Yes, I remembered Nicklaus asking me to marry him, and I remembered that I said yes. But I didn't connect it with speaking out loud. I felt my face burn red. I felt exposed. I, too, looked at the ground.

David continued, "I know that Nicklaus asked you to marry him, and I know you said yes. Shadow, I'm so sorry I didn't do more to save him!"

Tears hit the ground from his eyes and left small muddy droplets on the dusty path. I looked at him through my own tears and shook my head. I reached for his hand and held it in mine. I brought it to my lips and kissed it. Sweet David. He was carrying such a heavy and undeserved weight on his shoulders.

Our eyes met. David seemed to understand that I couldn't forgive him because there was nothing to forgive. He was responsible for saving the lives of so many that day. Nicklaus drowned, but it was no one's fault. Least of all David's. I managed a slight smile. David returned it.

Then he surprised me even further. He reached into his pocket and pulled out a little piece of folded material. As he unwrapped it, I saw a lock of sandy blond hair.

David said, "The day of Nicklaus's funeral, I took the scissors from Ma's sewing box—and the fabric, too. When I got to the church, I walked up to his coffin to pay my respects. I looked to be sure no one was watching, and I snipped a piece of his hair. I knew that no one else would do it for you since no one but me knows you were engaged. I don't have the money for a locket, but you should have his hair, at least."

He looked at the ground again.

After I caught my breath, I gave him another hug, took the fabric with Nicklaus's hair in it, and walked home with dry eyes. You see, I now had a piece of my love with me and always would.

I eventually bought a locket to put the hair in, and I wear it always. It hangs unseen under my collar and sits next to my heart.

As far as I know, David never told another soul that I spoke. He seemed to understand that my voice drowned that day by the lake along with all those others.

Kermit and Pius

It's late in the evening. Long past the time when decent folks should be sound asleep. But for me, dreams don't seem to want to come. I feel restless. This wind makes me nervous.

Every time I hear the wind blow like this, my thoughts turn to Kermit, Nicklaus's younger brother. It was blowing so hard the day he came to town that some of the roofs blew off houses. School closed because so many of the mothers thought it was too dangerous for the little ones to be out walking unattended. Those who did manage to get there, just had to hunker down in the little school house until the storm had calmed.

Esther Lindgren hung her laundry on her clothesline the night before. Most women wash their clothes in the morning and hang them to dry during the day. Then as evening comes on, they take the laundry in. But Mrs. Lindgren was a little unusual. She washed her family's clothes after the supper dishes were done. She could be seen hanging things on the line as the sun went down below the horizon. Then in the late morning, just before calling in the men for dinner, she would take the clothes down. She said she didn't like underclothes blocking her view of the prairie. The women gossiped about it sometimes, but everyone seemed to get used to her odd ways after a time.

The day Nicklaus's brother Kermit arrived, the Lindgren family's underclothes were blowing all over the township. The wind carried her husband's Sunday shirt a half mile up the road!

The extremely windy day of Kermit's arrival happened about a year after the tragic drownings. A few people still mentioned that day sometimes, but mostly everyone was trying to move on. The season's planting had just about finished. It was that short lull between planting and harvest when we felt we could catch our breath. You can't ever be lazy on the prairie, but once in a while you can relax a little.

Hulda and her youngest boy, Jack, who was about six then, had gone into town early that morning. They wanted to go to the post office, get some sugar, and stop by the mercantile for a pair of good work boots for Jack. As the youngest, Jack rarely got anything new. He wore the clothes that his older brothers outgrew and played with the toys the others weren't interested in any longer.

Jack was really excited about getting boots that had never been worn before. He told me that morning before breakfast, "Shadow, my feet won't know what to think! They've always had to take the shape of my brothers' feet, but now they can grow and move however they want!"

The wind started to come up when they were almost to town. Hulda said she thought about turning around and heading home. She could see the sky turning into dark swirling colors and knew a big storm was on its way. But Jack was so excited there was no use in even suggesting turning back. Once in town, they decided to ride out the storm at Noreen's Place with the others who found themselves stranded.

Noreen was a robust Irish woman who rented out three small rooms in the back of the house she shared with her brother. She also served meals to travelers and any local folks who stopped by at the right time of day. People didn't really like the food, but the place was conveniently located in the middle of town, close to the train station. No matter the hour, she always had a hot pot of coffee on the cook stove. The large front room with its stone fireplace served as a dining hall and was as good a place as any to gather and watch the people coming and going while you caught up on the town gossip. Which, of course, is one of the reasons Hulda loved to stop there when she was in town. The storm gave her a good excuse to settle in for a long, nosy visit.

Kermit and his friend Pius arrived on the train that afternoon and went straight to Noreen's Place to get their bearings. That's how Hulda and Jack happened to meet him that first day. Hulda told us all about it when they got home late that night.

If I close my eyes, I can see Hulda sitting at the table getting ready to tell us this bit of news. She still had on her "going to town" dress. It was navy blue with a little white flower pattern.

It had a high neck with a white ruffle at the wrists and hem. The storm caused her dark brown hair to look very unkempt despite the protection of her bonnet. Hulda took great care in her appearance, especially if she were going to town. But the wind had made it almost impossible to keep the tidy bun in place at the nape of her neck. She had big, bulging brown eyes that seemed to grow larger when she got excited about something, as she did that night. She resembled one of the bullhead fish we sometimes caught if our hook got too close to the bottom of the lake. Many years later we learned her bulging eyes were caused by a thyroid condition. But, of course, we didn't know that at the time.

Recalling that night at the supper table makes me homesick for those days long ago when I still lived with Herman and Hulda. There was always something to discuss over the table and I have to admit, I enjoyed listening to Jack challenge Hulda. I don't think there was another soul alive that she would tolerate if from. Truth be told, I believe she got a kick out of his back talk, even though she would never have admitted it.

Hulda began, "Well, you're not going to believe who Jack and I met at Noreen's today! As sure as I'm sittin' here, we met Nicklaus's brother Kermit and his friend, Pius! Let me tell you, it was somethin'."

Hulda poured herself a cup of coffee and settled back in her chair. We knew she was planning to take her time with this story.

And I was glad about it. The mention of my Nicklaus's name made me break out in a cold sweat. My stomach started doing flips, and my mouth instantly went dry. I couldn't even pretend to eat supper as Hulda spoke. Could it be true that his younger brother was actually nearby?

Hulda sipped her coffee and continued. "Well, as I said, after Jack and I left the mercantile, we decided to wait out the wind at Noreen's place."

Jack piped in, "Ma, we didn't decide anything. You were talking about stopping by Noreen's before we left this morning. We could've made it home. It was just wind, and it didn't even get bad 'til after we were already at Noreen's!"

Hulda scowled at him. "Hush up now, and quit sassing me, Jack. Let me tell 'em 'bout Nicklaus's brother." She continued, "Jack and I were sitting in Noreen's dining room in the back corner. You know that table I like? The one by the fire? It's really the best place to take everythin' in.

"I had just started talking to Clara about the cake she made for Mrs. Lindermann's funeral last week. I said to her, nice as you please, 'Clara, if you'd like my white frosted cake recipe, I'd be more'n happy to stop by some time and show you how I do it.' I was tryin' to be nice.

"Well, Clara seemed to take offense at this, and she says to me with that edge in her voice that she gets, 'Why on earth would I need your cake recipe, Hulda? I'm well known for my cinnamon coffee cake.'

"'Clara,' I said, 'you know it isn't right to serve coffee cake at a funeral! 'Specially one with cinnamon in it. Folks don't want cinnamon when they're grievin'. They want somethin' moist and comfortin' after the service.'

"She started arguin' with me then and said plenty o' people prefer her cinnamon coffee cake to my plain white cake. Can you imagine? I don't know where she gets these ideas! I actually saw the rev'rend stick his finger in my empty cake pan and lick up the crumbs off the bottom. Clara had to take almost half of hers back home, uneaten. Now, you tell me what 'plenty o' people' prefer!"

Hulda's eyes were big and getting bigger. Her cheeks started to redden, and we all knew that once she got going on something like this, she could go on for hours.

I was relieved when Herman finally said, "Hulda, we want to hear about Nicklaus's brother. Don't keep us waiting!" That brought her back to her story, and I was so thankful.

"Oh, all right, Herman," Hulda said. "As Clara and I were talkin', two young men walked in to the dining room. We didn't know them from Adam. The tall blonde didn't look to be twenty and carried only a small suitcase. I would guess the shorter man was a little older—say mid-twenties. He had almost black hair but a very light complexion that set off his hazel eyes so you really notice 'em. Those eyes were very striking.

"The tall blond man walked over to our table and took off his hat as the shorter one followed behind. He talked in a slow and careful way. I figure he was trying to hide his accent. 'Ma'am, my name is Kermit Haberer. I just got off the train, and I am hoping to find my cousin Kasper Schmidt's place. I do not think he is expecting me, but I am hoping he will agree to put me up until I can get settled. He did the same for my brother a while back.'

"I near fell off my chair. I asked, 'You don't mean to tell me you're Nicklaus's brother, do you?' I must have shouted the question because the crowded room got real quiet as everyone looked our way and leaned in to listen."

"Ya," Jack said, "the whole place went silent, and they all looked at us. It was like bein' in one of those scary stories Pa tells us sometimes when we're fishin'."

"Jack, I told you to hush so I can tell them about Nicklaus's brother, Kermit," Hulda said sharply. "Kermit seemed surprised that we all knew his brother. He said, 'Yes, ma'am, I am Nicklaus's little brother. Did you know him?'

"Did I know him? I thought. Why wouldn't I? He lived here and was homesteading along with the rest of us after all.

"So I said to him, 'Everyone 'round these parts knew your brother, young man. He was a pillar of our community, and there's more 'n one family that'll be indebted to him for his bravery and for their very lives, I might add. Once you get settled, you come find me, and I'll show you his tree I planted at the site of the tragedy.'"

As Hulda repeated what she said, her voice cracked some, and water welled in her eyes. The memory of that day by the lake was still so fresh.

I couldn't believe the story she was telling us. In addition to the cold sweat, I now had a lump in my throat that felt so big I would have sworn I swallowed an apple whole. I'd been privately mourning the loss of my Nicklaus and trying so hard to keep every moment we shared alive in my memory. Now there was someone in town who actually knew him when he was young. Who knew what he was like as a boy. His brother! His blood! I hung on every word that Hulda spoke.

"Lloyd Johnson was in Noreen's riding out the storm, and when he heard that Kermit was Nicklaus's brother, he whipped his neck 'round to get a look at him so fast and hard that I thought he was going to twist it right off his shoulders. The fool looked like an old barn owl."

Then, Hulda went on for a bit about how nosy he was and how his wife hadn't contributed to the church bake sale last month.

Herman was quick to interrupt her this time. He shot her a look and said, "Hulda, please!"

So Hulda continued, "When Kermit learned that so many knew Nicklaus and knew about him, too, because he was Nicklaus's little brother, he was a little taken aback. He said, 'Of course people here knew my brother. It just never occurred to me. I thought I was going to meet strangers. But, sitting here, listening to you all share stories about my brother, I feel like I'm meeting family.' He shook his head a little and looked at the floor. He was strugglin' to control his emotions."

"Are you kiddin' 'em now, Ma? He wasn't controllin' nothin'! He had big ol' tears runnin' down his face, and he didn't even try to hide 'em," Jack interrupted.

Hulda gave him a look. "Jack, if I have to tell you to hush one more time, you ain't gettin' those new boots even if you have to go barefoot!"

It went on like that for a while, so I'll just summarize Hulda's encounter the best I can.

It didn't take long before Noreen's Place had been transformed. Suddenly, there were two chairs brought out for the newcomers to sit on and the small crowd formed a misshapen circle around the men. They were the center of attention, and the group was eager to hear every word they said.

Kermit and his parents learned of Nicklaus's drowning from a letter sent by Cousin Kasper Schmidt. Kermit said he'd planned to come to Dakota and homestead with Nicklaus as soon as he turned eighteen. But his parents were now against the idea. They'd lost one son in America, and they sure weren't planning on losing the other. Kermit was not going to change his plans, though. In fact, he was more determined than ever. He had to see the place that took his brother's life with his own eyes. He knew it would be a difficult journey, but he believed that Nicklaus would somehow be with him to help him along the way.

On Kermit's eighteenth birthday, he waved good-bye to his family and made his way to the ship that would bring him across the water. On the ship he met Pius. When he got to Dakota Territory, Kermit was overwhelmed with emotion that his feet were standing on the same ground his brother's had just a year before.

As Hulda was talking, I was so focused on Kermit that I'd forgotten there were two men who walked into Noreen's that afternoon. Suddenly I was curious about Pius.

Unlike Kermit, Pius Kornder had no specific destination in mind. He planned to figure out his future once he landed in America. Pius was a quiet sort and let Kermit do most of the talking for him. He just nodded and smiled as Kermit told about how they met each other. Sometimes he added a comment or answered a direct question, but for the most part, he seemed happy to have Kermit speak for him. That's why even before I met him, I felt a kindred spirit in Pius.

Kermit and Pius had been assigned to the same bunk bed at the bottom of the ship. Kermit took the top and Pius the bottom. It was natural they'd become friendly, but according to Kermit, during the long confined journey, they became as close as brothers. They'd each set out for America alone, but once they found each other, they no longer had to feel lonely.

When Kermit learned that Pius had no kin waiting to help him, he suggested Pius join him in Dakota. He felt sure that Cousin Kasper Schmidt would find a way to take on one more for a short time. And so, there they were.

As the wind blew outside, the crowd at Noreen's asked questions and got familiar with the two men. Hulda said they were both nice young fellas and she was happy to meet them. It was also nice to have something to take their minds off the wind as it whipped through town all afternoon.

As evening came and the winds subsided, Hulda and Jack made their way back home.

Oh, and about Jack's boots: The mercantile didn't have boots in Jack's size, so he had to wait another month before the next shipment of supplies arrived. That night as I was tucking him into bed, he told me, "I don't want my feet thinking they have to grow into the shape of my bothers' feet. I want them to know they can grow into whatever shape they want to, no matter what Ma says!"

For the next few weeks, as soon as Hulda turned her back, he kicked his hand-me-down shoes off and went barefoot. Poor little Jack. It was a long month of waiting for him.

The following morning as Hulda and I were cleaning up the breakfast dishes and getting ready to start dinner, we saw Kermit and Pius walking toward the house.

"What in heaven's name?" Hulda gasped. "I look a mess. I wasn't expectin' company. Shadow you best start making another batch o' biscuits. Looks like we'll have two more for dinner. After all that travelin', they'll be hungry."

I was so nervous. I'd hardly slept a wink going over in my mind everything I'd heard about Kermit. I longed for a connection to my Nicklaus, and I was desperate to make a good first impression. I was sure Kermit wouldn't have heard anything about me, but I was so curious to see if he resembled the boy Nicklaus had described—the brother he missed so much.

Soon there was a knock at the door, and Hulda asked the two men to come in. I was so startled at my first sight of Kermit that I tripped on the broom that was propped against the wall and nearly fell head first onto the hot cook stove. It was the short, stout Pius who caught my arm and saved me from a terrible burn. I found myself staring into those surprisingly brilliant hazel eyes. No wonder Hulda had commented on them. I'd never seen eyes that color before.

Once I composed myself, I took a better look at Kermit. He looked back at me with a slight smile on his face. I felt my face turn red. I felt so clumsy. The look of recognition on his face as he watched me added to my embarrassment. He didn't have to say anything. The look on his face showed he knew me. It was quite unsettling, and it made me long to have my Nicklaus with me again. I wanted to ask Kermit what his brother told him about me. I forced myself to breathe deeply and force down the emotions that threatened to overcome me.

There was no mistaking that Kermit was Nicklaus's brother. Their features were different, and yet so similar. Well, let me correct that. There were similarities in their appearance for sure, but what was so surprising was the way Kermit moved. He moved and walked like Nicklaus, and when he sat in the chair, his shoulders slumped a little like his brother's had. Kermit even had that same funny way of looking at the floor before he asked you a question and then, when he was ready, he would look you in the eye so intently you felt he could almost read your thoughts. I took refuge on my little stool by the cook stove and tried to get control of myself.

Hulda immediately started battering the two with questions. She'd learned a lot about them at Noreen's the day before, but she obviously wanted more information. I knew she was anxious to pass along any new-found knowledge about these two young men to the nosy neighbors who would be sure to gather when they heard of their arrival.

Once they started talking amongst themselves, I felt a bit more comfortable and began preparing the extra food needed for dinner. After a bit, Hulda said it was time for the men to come in to eat. I went outside and rang the big triangle that hung from the roof of the house.

Herman and the boys must have been hungry because I could see them coming even before I hung the metal pipe back on the hook. Once they were all washed up and seated around the table, Kermit cleared his throat a little and looked down at his plate.

He said, "Me and Pius came here today for a purpose."

Then he looked Herman directly in the eyes and continued, "As you know, I met Pius on the ship. He didn't have any plans, so I told him he should come with me, and Cousin Kasper would help set us up. But, it turns out they don't have room for both of us. What with the new baby and his wife's family turning up, they're full. Kasper said I could sleep in the barn since I'm blood, but he couldn't see his way to put Pius up as well. So we was wondering if maybe you would consider letting Pius stay in your barn. It would only be until he got himself settled."

The table was quiet for a while. Herman looked at Kermit, then Pius. Finally his eyes met Hulda's. Hulda and Herman seemed to silently speak to each other with their stare. Finally the spell between them broke, and Hulda took a bite of food from her plate.

Herman said, "Pius, we would be happy to have you. Collect your belongings, and I can show you 'round when we get in from the field tonight. I 'spect we'll have to go over some things, but you seem like a nice enough fella. We got to know Nicklaus pretty well and treated him like family. Seein' how Kermit's his brother, we feel we can trust 'im. So if he vouches for you, that's good enough for us."

So that's how Pius came to live in the barn. Pius was a very quiet young man. He made a nice little place for himself in the loft of the barn. Since it was early summer, we didn't have to worry about keeping him warm. In fact, I don't know how he survived some of those hot, humid days that came on that season. I swear, sometimes the air gets so thick and heavy with humidity, I wonder how we don't all drown as we try to breathe it.

Pius didn't eat with the family. He said he didn't feel right about intruding in such a way. I think he was just really shy and didn't like the way Hulda would badger him with personal questions. It was just more peaceful in the barn.

Hulda couldn't see letting the poor young man go hungry out there in their barn. So she assigned me the chore of bringing him his supper each night. She'd dish up a big plate and set it aside before putting the food on the table for the others. Then, after we cleaned up the dishes, she'd send me out to the barn. Pius always ate everything on his plate. I'd sit and watch him eat. Hulda told me I was not to come back without his plate, so what was I to do? It was uncomfortable for me, and at first I don't think he liked my company, either. Since I don't talk and he hardly does, we mostly just stared at each other. I could definitely understand the desire to be quiet, but he was so quiet it made even me a bit restless.

These awkward silent dinners went on for a few weeks. Then one day Pius asked me a question. "Shadow, I know you don't talk, but do you read and write?"

I nodded eagerly. It was a treat to have the conversation.

"Well," he said, "I'd like to write a few letters. But I'm afraid I never learned to read or write. My pa passed when I was little, and I had to help my ma, so I didn't get a chance to go to school. Do you think you could do the writin' for me if I tell you what to say? It would mean a great deal to me."

I was so surprised. I'd never been asked to do something like that before. I felt so honored. I nodded eagerly and started to look around for a piece of paper and a pencil.

Pius guessed what I was looking for and started laughing. "I don't have any paper right now. I'll go to town tomorrow. I was afraid my request would be a burden on you, but I see you're as anxious to have this letter written as I am."

When he laughed, his hazel eyes seemed to glow. I realized all over again what a good-looking man he was.

All the next day, I looked forward to helping Pius. It would be nice to have something to do while I sat waiting for him to finish his supper. Plus, I've always liked to write.

I was lucky to be allowed to go to school. Hulda told Herman that she needed some time to herself once in a while. She said, "If Shadow would go to school, it would give me a nice break." I remember feeling hurt by those words. I knew she always felt I clung to her too closely, but I didn't know she disliked my presence that much. I mean, I tried to stay as quiet and out of the way as I could. But that was Hulda. She didn't hold back her thoughts or feelings. You just had to get used to her.

I liked school, and I got good grades. The school marms always complimented me on my penmanship. Writing was my favorite subject, and because most of the people in the village spoke German at home, we were taught both English and German in school. I could write well in either language.

As I tell you this, I wonder now why I didn't carry a piece of paper or pencil around with me. I wouldn't have had to speak to communicate. I could have just written my thoughts down.

As I think more about it, though, I guess I just never felt my thoughts were worth anyone's time. Plus, paper and pencils were a luxury that the family wasn't about to waste on me. And I never felt I had trouble communicating just as I was.

People tell me I have a very expressive face. I didn't need to talk to let a person know what I was thinking. He just understood. After I lost my Nicklaus by the lake, I decided it would be best if I didn't talk again. It seemed right that Nicklaus was the last one to hear my voice. So that's that.

Anyway, I should get back to the story. As I was pulling weeds that afternoon in the vegetable garden, I realized that I didn't know if Pius wanted the letter written in German or English. This was a problem. Since I don't speak, I thought I could write the question on the piece of paper that Pius was going to get. But Pius doesn't read. So how would I be able to know which language he wanted the letters to be written in?

I decided the best way to solve the problem was to write the question for Kermit to read. Then Kermit could ask Pius, and all would be answered.

Pius helped Herman with the field on occasion, but for the most part, he spent his days with Kermit working on the house.

Kermit decided he would complete the homestead that Nicklaus had claimed. The barn was already almost finished, and it made sense that his brother would live on the place.

Since Cousin Kasper Schmidt was the only relative around, everyone just assumed his place would be claimed by him after Nicklaus drowned. But Cousin Kasper seemed happy to turn it over to Kermit. I overheard Kasper's wife tell Hulda one day after church, "The young man is nice enough, but he has an odd manner. Our house is full to capacity, and with him living in the barn, it's just too much."

Hulda was curious. "Odd manner, you say. What do you mean by that? He's not a drinker, is he?"

Mrs. Schmidt smiled. "No, Hulda, I don't think he has even mentioned spirits since he's been here, and we sure don't allow that kind of thing in our house—or barn, for that matter. I really shouldn't have said anything. He just has an odd way, that's all. Nothing bad. But I'll be glad when he has his own place. Let's just leave it at that."

"Humph," Hulda said. I knew she wanted to know more, and sure enough, she invited Kermit for dinner that very afternoon. He declined the invitation, though. He said that he and Pius were going to spend the nice afternoon fishing in the pond.

Hulda was grumpy the rest of the day.

Kermit told Pius that if he helped him get the place finished, he could live there with him. Nicklaus designed the house to be a story-and-a-half soddie. It was going to be bigger than most of the sod houses in town, but he wanted a bedroom on the main floor big enough to fit a bed for the two of us and a little crib for a baby. He was planning to make the little upstairs big enough for two beds so several more children could sleep comfortably.

I remember how I blushed when he told me about his plans. He hadn't even asked me to marry him at that point, and he was already talking about sharing a bed with me and about the babies we would have.

I often wonder how different my life would be if Edith Schoenmann hadn't lost those false teeth that day.

Anyway, as I was saying, I stopped weeding the garden and motioned to Hulda that I was going for a walk.

She sighed. "Oh, all right. You been workin' hard 'nough on this hot day. You might as well take a little break. But don't be gone too long. I'm gonna need some help with supper."

I made my way to Kermit and Pius' place. It was only about a mile up the road, so it didn't take me long.

When I walked up to the place, I was shocked at how far the two had gotten. The first floor of the sod house was complete, and they'd started on the half story. It was quite remarkable. You could tell these men knew what they were doing. They already had several windows and a door in place, and the walls were really talking shape. They'd rented a new machine from the mercantile called a grasshopper that cut through the thick prairie grass to make strips twelve inches wide and four inches thick. From those strips they cut three-foot bricks using a corn knife. They stacked the bricks in alternating layers lengthwise and crosswise. This made for a sturdy wall that could hold the heat from a cook stove on those bitterly cold, windy winter days.

Kermit and Pius had even built a little two-windowed shed about fifty yards off. The outhouse had been dug already, and the building on top completed. It wouldn't be long now before they'd be ready to move in.

As I approached, I heard the two men talking and laughing. I couldn't make out what they were saying, but it made me glad to hear them so happy at their labor. I walked up to the new door and gave a little knock. Suddenly the talking stopped, and I could hear some shuffling around. In a minute or so Kermit opened the door.

He smiled. "Come in, Ray. Nice to see you here."

When I heard him call me by the name Nicklaus gave me, the air seemed to leave my lungs. I suddenly felt very cold and started to sweat at the same time. I looked for a chair to sit on, and when I didn't see one in the empty house, I sat right down on the hard-packed dirt floor. I could feel the color drain from my face, and it took me a few moments to compose myself. I knew Kermit recognized me as Nicklaus's girlfriend, but I wasn't prepared to hear him call me the name he'd given me. How did he know? How much had Nicklaus told him about me?

Hearing someone call me Ray stirred so many emotions. I started to cry a little as I sat there on the floor. When I finally got myself under control enough, I looked up to see both Kermit and Pius standing over me with horror on their faces.

Pius said, "Shadow, are you alright? What in heaven's name happened to you? I'll get you some water. Just sit there and don't move."

As Pius left the house to go to the well, Kermit started talking very fast. "I'm so sorry I startled you like that. It's because I called you Ray, isn't it? Even though they called you Shadow, I recognized you that first day when Pius and me was over at Herman's place. I didn't say anything about it because—well, Hulda kept batterin' me with all those questions. Nicklaus always called you Ray in his letters, so I just think of you as Ray. Now I feel terrible. I'm such a fool! Please! Forgive me! I'm an oaf! Just sit there a minute. Here's Pius now with some water."

Pius handed me the tin cup filled with cool well water. "Here, Shadow, drink this. But slowly. You had some sort of spell, I guess." Then to Kermit, he said, "What the heck is going on? Why did you call her that?"

Kermit explained that his brother Nicklaus was in love with me and was planning to propose as soon as the house was finished. He told Pius all about my courtship with Nicklaus. He even brought up details I'd almost forgotten. It was nice to listen to these stories and know that Nicklaus loved me as I loved him. But it was a bit unsettling, too. Though for the most part I liked the way Kermit described Nicklaus's feelings for me. It made it all seem real again.

Then Kermit said, "Ray, I have something for you. It was in with Nicklaus's things. Cousin Kasper said he saved all of my brother's belongings after the drowning without knowing why. When I turned up, he told me he was glad he hadn't tossed them. I just need to run out to the shed."

I really had never thought about Nicklaus's things. How odd that it hadn't occurred to me that he had personal belongings. Grief is a funny thing, I guess.

Kermit returned with a little leather-bound book. He told us that it was Nicklaus's journal. He recalled how, when he discovered it, he stayed up all night and read every word. He finally fell asleep just before dawn and slept right through breakfast. Kermit said the last entry was just two sentences. "Tomorrow is Sunday. I plan to ask Ray if she can spend the afternoon with me."

I had no idea that Nicklaus wrote down his thoughts. The preciousness of these pages was almost more than I could bear. I was glad I was still sitting on the floor. I held my breath as Kermit opened it to the page he'd marked.

He began to read.

I miss my family terribly and think of them often. I am doing well and working hard to make a life for myself here. Cousin Kasper has taken me in, and he and his wife are helping me get myself set up. I sure do miss Ma's cooking, though. Mrs. Schmidt is a bit lacking in that area. I don't want to appear ungrateful, though. I really do appreciate what they are doing for me.

I haven't been to church yet but plan to go on Sunday.

But the most amazing thing happened today. I can't hardly believe this, but I met the girl I'm going to marry today! I know if I said this to Pa, he would probably roll his eyes and laugh. I can see him now saying, "That boy will never settle down with just one girl. He'll chase as many as he can as long as he can and end up alone." But this girl is different.

I was in town walking down Main Street thinking about the land I just bought and where I would start to build. I happened to look over toward the post office, and there she was. The most beautiful girl I ever laid eyes on. It rained yesterday, and I could see that her shoes were all muddy and her skirt was wet and stuck to her legs. But I swear it only made her prettier. She has long, *thick brown hair. It's the color of a cinnamon stick. Light brown with just a little gold when the light hits it just right. And she has these big brown eyes. They're so dark you can hardly see her pupils. Her skin is a light olive color, and she has the cutest hooked nose with a little bump on the top. Her nostrils are flared like she's sniffing something wonderful. <u>I have never seen a more beautiful creature in all my life.</u>*

Well, I stopped dead in my tracks. I usually don't hesitate to go talk to a pretty girl, but this time was different. Somehow this time, I felt pressure to make a good impression. I was nervous, but I swallowed hard and walked right up to her and introduced myself.

As I spoke, the most fantastic thing happened. Her cheeks started to glow this wonderful rosy color. Her eyes seemed to speak to me. It was then that I noticed her mouth. She has this really full bottom lip and the top is thin but almost makes a heart shape. She is incredible, really.

As I was introducing myself, this funny little boy named David came up and told me she didn't talk. He seemed to act as her guardian or something. I could see he was sweet on her and didn't want to let me get close to her. So I did what Uncle Krause used to do to me and Kermit when he wanted to get rid of us. He would tell us he was going to time us and make us run somewhere. Before we could protest, he would say real loud, "One, two, three,

GO!" and we would run our tails off. It worked like a charm today, just like it did back home.

With David gone, I was able to talk to this angel alone. David was right. She doesn't speak, but we didn't have any trouble. Those eyes and that face say so much she doesn't need to make a sound. I could have sat there all day with her.

David told me they call her Shadow. I think that name is a crime. It sounds like something you would name a horse, not the name of the most glorious girl in the whole world. So I told her I was going to call her Ray because she reminded me of a ray of sunshine. She seemed to like the idea.

I'm planning to call on her tomorrow. I'm so nervous. I hope she likes me.

As Kermit read from the journal, I felt so strange. I was transported back in time to the moment we met. I had no idea what was going through Nicklaus's mind that day. He seemed so confident. He told me many times he thought I was beautiful, but I didn't understand what he was talking about. I used to look in the mirror but never saw what Nicklaus did. Hearing Kermit read the description was very unsettling. I longed to see Nicklaus again. The pain of losing him seemed fresher than ever. I wondered if I would ever get over him.

Of course, now I know that I never will. Nicklaus was the best man I ever met and ever will meet. I've learned to live with the loss, but I'm sure I will never get used to living without him.

Kermit handed me the book. He said, "Ray, I'd like you to have this. He mentioned you with such affection in the letters he wrote to us. We knew you were someone very special to turn my brother's head, and once I read his diary, I understood. My family and I will forever be grateful that he found someone to love before he left this earth. Thank you."

I held the diary close. Well, more like gripped it. Looking at it and seeing my Nicklaus's handwriting made me dizzy. I'd never seen his handwriting, yet as I looked at the shape of the letters, I felt him so strongly. I even brought the journal to my face and smelled it. Of course, if Nicklaus's scent was ever on the paper, it had long ago dissipated, but seeing his handwriting made him more than a memory. Nicklaus was real.

Tears streamed uncontrolled down my face as I looked up to see those two young men overcome with emotion as well. We must have been quite the sight sitting there in that empty room on that dirt floor. That moment bonded us, and we became close friends from that afternoon on.

Kermit and Pius talked about Nicklaus for a time. I loved sitting there listening to them talk about my relationship. And learning things about him from his brother that I never knew before. Being in the presence of someone who missed him as much as I did was an unexpected comfort. It was a beautiful afternoon.

Suddenly I remembered that I had come for a purpose. I motioned to Pius and made a gesture of someone writing. He nodded and grabbed a crisp piece of paper from the new pack he'd just bought and a freshly sharpened pencil.

I wrote, "Does Pius want the letters in German or English?" and handed the paper to Kermit.

Kermit had a puzzled look on his face when he read the note. He then looked at Pius and read it aloud. Pius' face colored as he looked at the floor.

Kermit said, "Pius, does this mean you can't read?

"Yes," Pius mumbled.

No one spoke for at least a minute. Finally, Kermit broke the silence. "Pius, I don't understand why you would ask Ray to write a letter for you. Why not me?" He seemed hurt.

Pius looked up as if shamed. "Well, it's just that I didn't want you to think I was stupid. I knew Shadow, uh Ray, wouldn't tell anyone that I can't read or write. I thought maybe I could keep it a secret. I don't want you to think less of me. But I need to let my family know that I'm alive and well here in Dakota."

With irritation, Kermit said, "Pius, I know you're not stupid. I can't believe you think I'm so small-minded. After all we went through to get here, I thought you knew me better than that. I need to go for a walk." With that he turned and left the house.

Pius looked at me. My face must have shown the guilt I felt for exposing his secret. I never dreamed that it even was a secret. Especially from Kermit. They were so close and spent so much time together. I felt awful. I knew in that moment I must always do a better job of keeping the things people share with me to myself. I didn't ever want to be the cause of someone else's pain again.

Pius managed a weak smile, and his beautiful hazel eyes sought mine. He looked directly at me and said, "Ray, it's all right. This is my fault, not yours. I should have told Kermit long ago. I should have told you that no one else knew. I really don't know why I feel so ashamed about it. I mean, over half the township can't read or write. It's just that I care what Kermit thinks of me."

I looked at Pius and then at the door that Kermit left through. I gave Pius a pained look. I wanted him to go and look for Kermit.

Pius smiled slightly as he guessed my thought, "No, Shadow, I've learned that when he says he needs some time, the best thing is to give it to him. He can be moody, but he always comes around. I'll talk to him when he gets back. He'll be okay."

It was then that I recalled Mrs. Kasper Schmidt telling Hulda about Kermit's odd manner. I guessed this moodiness was what she was talking about.

I looked at the note and then at Pius. Pius chuckled, "Oh, to answer your question, this first letter can be written in German. There will be a few others in English. I'll remember to tell you which language before you start each letter. Well, that is if you would agree to write more than one."

I sensed that Pius still felt upset because Kermit had become so angry with him. But before he could say anything more, Regina, Hulda and Herman's daughter, burst through the door. I don't remember her knocking or anything. She was out of breath. She said, "Shadow, you got to get home and quick. Ma is fit to be tied. She found out you've been over here all afternoon without a chaperone, and she's mad as a wet hen!" Then, she turned to Pius and gave him a little wink and smoothed her hair. Even at the age of thirteen, Regina was a shameless flirt.

I realized then how long I'd been away. I stood up, nodded, and left. Regina and I half walked, half ran back home. As we made our way, Regina said she was out picking raspberries and saw me go to Kermit's place. She innocently told Hulda when she asked her if she'd seen me. Regina felt awful for getting me in trouble.

Hulda was waiting for us. She started yelling at me before I was even completely through the door. She said that young single girls had no business spending the afternoon alone with a couple of bachelors. She asked me what people would think and did I want them calling me a hussy?

This went on until Herman finally stopped her. He said in his low, quiet voice, "Hulda, can't you see she's had enough? What's done is done. Now, let's eat."

Herman had a way with Hulda. I don't know if it was the look on his face or the tone of his voice, but he could always get her to stop one of her tirades. I knew she was right, though. It just wasn't proper for a girl to be alone with two young men like that. I didn't do anything wrong, but I knew how people could talk. I hardly ate a bite that night. I felt sick to my stomach.

After supper, I was still feeling pretty ashamed about my behavior as we were cleaning up the dishes.

When Hulda's back was turned, Regina whispered in my ear, "Don't worry, Shadow. I won't say anything. Ma won't either. Just don't do it again." Then she gave me a little squeeze on my arm and winked at me.

It did make me feel better, but I knew I had to be more careful. I wasn't a little girl any more.

That night, Jack was told to come with me to bring Pius his supper.

"Aw, come on, Ma! Why do I always have to go? Can't I just relax once?" Jack complained.

Hulda shot back, "Relax? What in heaven's name have you been doing all day that you need to relax? You'll do as you're told, and that's the last of it!"

"But, Ma, I don't want to. I'm wore out from pickin' all those beans. Can't you send Regina?"

"No, I can't send your sister," Hulda said with exasperation. "This whole mess is my fault for sending Shadow out there unattended in the first place. I don't know what I was thinking. Lord knows what people would say if that ever got out!"

Herman piped in, "Jack, enough of your sass. You heard your Ma. Get your boots on now. Pius' supper is gettin' cold."

Jack did as he was told and followed me to the barn, mumbling and grumbling the whole way.

When we climbed up to the loft with the food, Pius couldn't hide his surprise at seeing Jack. "Well, what do we have here? I'm gettin' extra comp'ny tonight with my supper! What brings you out tonight, Jack?"

Jack sighed deeply, "Geez, Lord knows I didn't want to come! No offense, Pius, but Ma is all worked up in the house tonight, and instead of takin' it easy like I should be, I'm walkin' all the way out here to watch you eat! She thinks you and Shadow are gonna get in some kinda trouble together because you're a boy and she's a girl." He sighed again. "But I'm a boy, too. Somehow if there are two boys and a girl it's okay. I don't understand what the heck's goin' on!"

Pius looked at me and winked, which made my face burn. "Well, Jack, I'm happy to have you. I hope you don't mind, but Shadow and I have some work to do tonight."

"Well, if you think I'm gonna help, you can think again!" Jack squawked. "I been workin' all day, and I need some time for myself!"

Pius laughed, "No, Jack, you just sit back and take your rest. Shadow and I are gonna write some letters. You might as well know, I never learned to read or write, so she's gonna help me."

"Well, lots o' folks can't read and write," Jack shot back. "I don't know why I gotta be here 'cause of that!"

"That isn't why you're here, Jack," replied Pius. "Someday it will make sense to you, but for now your only job is to sit back and make yourself comfortable."

With that Pius gave me the crisp new paper and a sharpened pencil. It was a bit of an awkward start. I expected Pius to tell me exactly what to write, but instead he started like this:

"Okay, the first letter should be in German. It's going to my parents. You can start by letting them know I made it here all right. Tell them I met Kermit, and he told me about Dakota Territory. You can tell them that I'm helpin' him build his house, and he's gonna let me live there until I can get my own place. Tell them the people are nice here."

Instead of writing, I just looked blankly at him. Did he expect me to come up with the actual sentences? As he paused and waited for me to start, I quickly understood that was exactly what he had expected. So I put up my hand for him to pause. I thought about what I would want my own mother and father to know if I could write to them. So I wrote this in German:

Dear Mama and Papa,

I have asked a friend of mine to write you this letter. I know you must be wondering where I am and if I made it to America. I am so happy to tell you that I arrived safely and have made my way to a place called Dakota Territory. I met a man named Kermit on the ship, and upon his invitation, I am planning to settle here. The prairie is beautiful! It is so flat you can see for miles, and the sky goes on forever. There are wildflowers in the fields, and the ground is fertile. Thanks to the lack of trees on this prairie, the only obstacle to planting is the rocks. But we don't mind them too much. The people use those rocks to build fences and make the foundations of their homes stronger. We just get them out of the way before we plow. Kermit and I are building a house made of sod, and it is going to be really beautiful. I will live with him until I can earn enough to get myself set up. I have made many friends in

this community, and they have become like a second family to me.
We help each other in so many ways. It makes the hard work very
enjoyable. I am happy here, and I think I will be very successful.

I didn't know if Pius would like what I wrote. It was nice to have Jack with us because I handed him the letter and motioned for him to read it.

"Hey! Pius said all I had to do was get comfortable," Jack complained. "Just when I get situated, you ask me to read. This isn't fair!"

Pius said, "Please, Jack, it would mean a lot to me."

Jack sighed deeply and read the letter aloud. He was very clever and learned to read and write in both German and English so quickly that he was placed three grades above the others his age. He had a passion for learning and Hulda often found him hiding somewhere reading rather than doing his chores.

As he read, I watched Pius' face to see his reaction. His hazel eyes flew wide open, and by the time Jack finished, his mouth hung loose. I didn't know what to think of his reaction. But before I knew what was happening, he pushed his dinner plate aside and jumped up and gave me a hug.

I flushed hot. This was exactly the type of thing that Hulda wanted to avoid. I was stunned by his advance and stiffened immediately. Jack was looking at us, and I was so embarrassed I could have crawled under a hay bale.

Pius said, "Oh my, Shadow. I'm sorry. I was just so overcome with the letter. Those words were exactly what I wanted, but I didn't know how to say them. My mama will be so comforted. Thank you so much!"

I looked at Jack, wondering what he would say. His only response was, "Gosh, Shadow." I didn't know what that meant.

I wrote a few more paragraphs for Pius, and then Jack and I went back to the house with the dishes. I was so afraid that Jack would tell Hulda about the hug. I had come to enjoy the evening visits with Pius, and I didn't want her to forbid me from spending time with him.

I didn't have to worry, though. Jack started complaining immediately about how tired he was and how we made him read a stupid letter and how he didn't want to have to do this every night.

Hulda shot back, "You will go tomorrow night and every night after, young man!"

Not much else was said that night by anyone. We all stepped lightly. It was nights like this that the slightest thing could set Jack and Hulda to fighting, and we all knew it. That stubborn, opinionated mother and her youngest son were so very much alike.

The next day, I went over to Theophil's place. Lydia asked for my help to make raspberry jam. I loved helping Lydia. Their house had just as many people in it now as Hulda and Herman's, but it didn't feel the same. There was a calm there. A sort of quiet peace. Lydia seldom scolded her children. She didn't really have to. They just seemed to understand what needed to be done and did it without complaint. There was always laughter in that house as well. As you know, Theophil liked to tell stories, and a couple of his boys developed the same habit. Lydia's house certainly wasn't as clean and orderly as Hulda's, but no one seemed to notice or mind.

As I said, I was helping Lydia put up the raspberries. The men had just finished their lunch, and we were cleaning up the sticky red juice and sugar that had bubbled over on the cook stove. Jack knocked on the door. He was looking for Theophil and Lydia's third son, Karl. The two boys were the same age and planned to spend the afternoon fishing.

"Come on in, Jack," Lydia greeted, "and have a slice of bread with this jam we're makin'. You can tell us if it's any good."

Finally, a job I don't mind doin'! I'll have two pieces if ya got 'em," Jack replied.

"I been working myself silly lately," Jack complained with his mouth full of jam and bread. "Ma even has me working after supper now!"

Theophil and Lydia exchanged a smile that had so much love and understanding in it. When I saw these little glimpses of their adoration for each other, I'd often remember Theophil's dark time more than twenty years back and how Lydia had wiped all that sadness away just by showing up. It was magical.

Theophil turned to Jack. "Well, what the heck does she have you doin' after supper?"

Jack swallowed. "Ma has it in her head that I have to go with Shadow to watch Pius eat at night. She said if I don't go, people are gonna start talkin', and she won't have it. Then when I get out there, I have to read these letters Shadow's writin' for him. I mean, the letters are nice and all, but my eyes get heavy after dark."

Theophil and Lydia both turned to look at me. "You're writin' letters, Shadow?" Theophil asked.

I could feel my cheeks reddening. I nodded and looked at the floor.

Lydia said to Jack, "I didn't know she did that. How did that come about?"

Jack replied, "Like I said, they're just letters, but boy does she make 'em sound nice. When I read the first one, I wished it wasn't so late so I could've enjoyed it more. But Ma has me running from sunup to sundown. I can't find a minute for myself!"

With that, Jack and Karl went fishing, and Theophil headed out to help the boys in the field. Lydia and I finished up the jam, and I walked back home. I thought that would be the end of the conversation about my letter writing.

I should have known better. People like to gossip, and the fact that I was writing letters for Pius was all the talk at church on Sunday. At first Hulda was upset. She thought the ruckus was about me being alone and unchaperoned with a young man. But that's not what they were talking about at all.

Pius had shown Kermit the letter, and he started bragging about me to everyone he could. Jack kept interrupting him to make sure everyone knew he was there when I wrote the letter and was the first one to read it aloud. I felt so uncomfortable with everyone talking about me that I wished Pius had never asked me to write for him.

Not long after that, though, people started asking me to write letters for them, too. At first it was just folks who never learned to read or write like Pius. But then I started getting requests from others. They wanted me to describe their flower gardens or the accomplishments of their children. Sometimes they were proud of a barn or a cow. More than once a young man asked me to write to the girl who had caught his eye. I took care to say exactly what they wanted me to say and nothing more. Sometimes it was awkward because they wanted me to stretch the truth.

For instance, one young man hired a photographer to take a picture of him in a suit sitting at a desk. He planned to send the picture along with one of my letters to a lady he met on the train. He told me he wanted her to think he was a prosperous man of business. But the truth was, he was a farmer like almost everyone else in these parts. I pretended to have a headache and stopped writing.

He caught on and didn't ask me to finish. I learned later that he sent the photograph to the woman without the letter but never got a response.

I still write letters for people to this day. Now it's usually a birthday wish or a note on a special occasion. In exchange for these letters, I used to get things like a chicken or a pie, but these days I usually get a few dollars or a hotdish of some sort and sometimes a little material for sewing or some chopped wood. The people in these parts take care of me. I don't know why they give me so much for such a small thing, but I'm certainly grateful.

Looking back, I'm proud of myself for writing all those letters, and I'll always be grateful to Pius for getting me started. It allowed someone like me to live a good life on my own.

Pius…I do miss him. And Kermit, too. So let me return to their story.

Not long after I wrote those first letters, Pius and Kermit finished the house and moved in together as planned. Jack said he was relieved he didn't have to walk out to the barn every night, but I think he missed Pius' company all the same. I know I did.

The day they moved in was another windy day. I remember it well because the little housewarming party they planned almost didn't happen.

The two men had invited the Kasper Schmidt family, Hulda, Herman, and the rest of us over for a dinner. They bought a pig to butcher and were planning to cook a large ham. Hulda filled her biggest bowl with fresh green beans and a little bacon for flavor. She even baked one of her famous white frosted cakes for dessert. We'd heard Mrs. Kasper Schmidt would be bringing a whole kettle of her buttery mashed potatoes and several dozen ears of fresh corn on the cob. We were salivating all day thinking about the feast.

Late that afternoon the wind came up. It started to whip the newly fallen leaves all around. The skies didn't look threatening, but Herman was nervous about the animals getting out if the fence blew over. He told the boys to stay home, but Jack wasn't about to be left behind. Instead of risking another argument between Jack and Hulda, Herman told Hulda we should bring Jack along to help carry the beans. So, Herman, Hulda, Regina, Jack, and I decided to head out. It wasn't a long distance to the little house, and we were really looking forward to that ham.

Walking against the wind, it took us twice as long as it should have. Actually, something besides the wind slowed us down. A little mishap occurred along the way.

As Jack was carrying the pot of beans, the wind caught the lid, and it flew off. It hit Regina's arm. She screamed out in pain, Jack fell to the ground laughing, I dived to catch the pot of beans before it tipped over, and Hulda set to yelling at us all. By the time we got to Kermit's place, we were a dusty, windswept mess.

Kasper's bunch had it easier. The wind bore them along, and by the time we got there, they were all settled at the table drinking cider. I was amazed at how the house had taken shape. It was exactly as my Nicklaus had described it to me. He would have been so proud of his brother. Looking around, warmed by the cozy fire, I grew teary-eyed as I longed for what could have been. I missed him so much that night.

When I was able to push back my sadness, I noticed the furniture for the first time. The whole party was admiring the detailed and beautiful pieces. The legs on the tables were curved, and the chair backs were ornately carved. I'd never seen anything like them. The blanket chest even had a prairie scene carved into the top. The kitchen table top had been waxed to such a sheen that I could actually see my reflection.

None of us knew Pius was a furniture maker. He'd ordered the wood from the North Woods of Minnesota, and it had arrived on the train in several shipments. As it turned out, the little shed on the other side of the house was Pius' workshop. He had created all of this right on the property. It was beautiful.

As everyone was complimenting him and asking him questions about this piece and that, he called our attention to the top of a little side table. "I saw this carved in one of the logs, and I couldn't bring myself to cover it up. At first the carving was so weathered I could barely make it out. I used a special technique to add contrast to the wood. Look what it says."

We all bent over and got a close look. We could clearly see a carved heart. Inside it we read, 'Jared loves Lally.' I still have that table, and often wonder who Jared and Lally were and what circumstances occurred to make him proclaim his love in this way. How did that piece of wood end up in Dakota all the way from the North Woods? It was sweet of Pius to preserve it with his artistry.

Word quickly spread about Pius' furniture. As new families arrived, he kept very busy making tables, chairs, and beds to fill their homes. For a time, there wasn't a baby born among us who didn't sleep in a cradle Pius made. His craftsmanship was so fine that many of these cradles were passed down from generation to generation. I know for a fact that in the Olson family, five generations have slept in one of his cradles.

With Pius busy making furniture and Kermit busy in the field. We didn't see too much of them that fall. I'm sure Pius had earned enough to buy his own place, but the two men got along very well and neither seemed in any hurry to change the arrangement.

Regina had her eye on Pius. As I said earlier, she was a shameless flirt. She invented all sorts of reasons to head over to their place (with Jack or one of the other boys in tow, of course). Sometimes it was to get an ingredient for something she was baking. Other times, it was to help a friend pick out the style of chair that would best fit in her home. After church on Sundays, fifteen-year-old Regina would make a beeline over to Pius and laugh at everything he said whether it was meant to be funny or not.

The whole business caused much anxiety for Hulda. She watched Regina like a hawk and made sure that she was never left alone with Pius.

One day I saw Kermit in town. We were both heading home, and he asked if he could walk with me. I nodded. It was nice to have company, and I missed both Kermit and Pius. I was careful to keep an appropriate distance as we walked, though. I didn't want anyone talking about me the way they were starting to talk about Regina.

Kermit talked as we walked. He wanted to know if I knew Regina had been spending time at their place. I nodded. I think the whole town knew she was sweet on Pius.

Kermit lamented, "I don't see why she feels the need to be so brazen where Pius is concerned. It isn't becoming of a girl her age. Or a girl of any age for that matter. I don't know why Pius doesn't just tell her to stop. I actually think he likes it! I told him I didn't think he should encourage her like that, but he just smiled and walked out to his furniture shed. I swear, sometimes I get so mad! I haven't spoken to him in a couple of days, and yesterday I burned his toast on purpose. I don't know how to get through to him. I hope someone can convince him to steer clear of her before it's too late. Lord knows he won't listen to me."

I didn't really understand where his anger was coming from. Regina was flirtatious, but she had a very loving heart. Besides being a hard worker when she put her mind to something, she was beautiful. True, there was a large age difference between them, but that sort of thing was common in those days. I could see no reason that Pius shouldn't fall in love with her. I gave Kermit a puzzled look.

Kermit seemed angered at my response. He humphed. "See, no one understands. This is useless. If you don't mind, I'm going to walk home the long way. Take care, Ray."

I was stunned. The whole conversation reminded me again of Mrs. Kasper Schmidt's comment, "He has an odd manner."

When Pius didn't show interest, it didn't take long for Regina to turn her attention to another. She didn't stop her pursuit of Pius, but she had a difficult time remaining focused on just one man. If Pius had given her even a little bit of hope, things might have turned out better for Regina. She didn't know it then, but she was heading toward a very difficult time. I will tell you more about Regina soon enough. This is Pius and Kermit's story, and I don't want to get off track.

The year everything changed for Kermit and Pius wasn't particularly remarkable. As it does every year, fall turned to winter. The wind blew, and the skies turned gray. I do remember a couple things, though.

That season, the snows came slowly at first. We didn't have snow on Thanksgiving, and by Christmas there was only about a foot on the ground. It was plenty cold, though. The wind was relentless. It whipped what little snow had fallen into ground blizzards. Lydia and I were riding out one of these storms at Noreen's Place when David walked in.

He came right over and asked if he could join us. He seemed a bit shaken. When he left his place that morning, he could see for miles from the top of the hill. But as he walked down, the visibility became worse and worse until he worried he wouldn't make it to town. But he was afraid to turn back for fear he'd get lost in the white-out and not find his way home.

Lydia told him it was good that he came to Noreen's. He should ride out the storm with us, she said. The winds usually calm as the sun goes down, and that's just what they did that day.

As we sat quietly by the fire drinking our coffee and listening to the wind howl outside, I thought about how much

David had grown in the three years since my Nicklaus was taken from me. David was now sixteen and was beginning to look more like the man he would become rather than the boy that he'd been.

Shortly after New Year's Day, the weather warmed some. This was a welcome reprieve from the bitter cold, but with the warmer temperatures came more snow. By the end of January, at least three feet of snow lay on the ground. I love the way the gray days of heavy snowstorms open into brilliantly clear mornings with the snow twinkling in the fields like sugar. Everything looks so clean and new. It provides hope for the soul.

The warmer temperatures made the snow perfect for a snowman. Pius and Kermit must have had a touch of cabin fever because the two built a whole giant snow family in their front yard. It was the talk of the township, and several families made a special trip out there to see it after church. It was nice to have a happy diversion in the middle of winter.

The week before Valentine's Day, we were busy in the house putting the finishing touches on our new clothes for the barn dance which was to be held over at Theophil's place. Theophil loved having a crowd gather in the last days of winter. He said it was good to shake out the cold and produce some heat with plenty of dancing. He believed it would help bring on the spring.

Each year, Theophil, Lydia, and their family would clean out a space in the barn and set up tables for food. Several of the neighbors would create a makeshift band with a fiddle or two and at least a couple accordions. Occasionally someone would sing, but most often it was just music without lyrics. The dance was something we all looked forward to. The women made everyone in their family a new outfit for the event.

It stormed terribly for three days the second week of February that year. The wind continued its relentless howl day and night, not stopping as it usually did when the sun went down. The sound kept waking me up all night long. Snow fell heavily for three straight days as well. Herman told the boys to string a rope from the house to the barn so they wouldn't get lost in the white-out on their way to and from feeding the livestock.

Hulda, Regina, and I were inside busily preparing baked goods and sewing our clothes for the dance, but cold drafts found their way through the thick sod walls.

As the storm let up on the fourth day, David stopped by in the late morning. The whole family was in the house. The boys had just come in from their early chores, and Regina and I were helping Hulda get lunch started. We'd all been confined indoors too long during the storm, and our nerves were on edge.

After we invited David in, we crowded into the kitchen, relieved to have someone new to talk to. We were all standing, except for Hulda, who sat with David at the table. When Hulda asked him what brought him out so soon after the storm, David stared at the floor. By the look on his face, we all knew the reason wasn't good.

I poured him a cup of coffee and put a few biscuits on a plate with the jar of raspberry jam beside it so he could help himself. David was a big eater, and even with the heavy news he was about to share, he gobbled down a biscuit with a generous amount of jam before he started. He paused as he took a sip of the hot coffee. He stared at his plate as if summoning his strength to continue.

"Well," he said, "Ma sent me over here to tell you all the news. I ain't gonna lie: It's bad. Pius has gone missing."

The town formed a search party to look for Pius. Of course, the central point of the search had to be Kermit's place since it was the last place anyone had seen him. If he'd gotten lost in the storm, he couldn't have gone far. But with all the new snow on the ground, there was no way to know what direction he went. We had no way to track him.

Hulda organized the women, and we took over Kermit's place. Instead of dancing at Theophil's on Valentine's Day, we kept vigil at Kermit's. For days on end we did our part, baking, cleaning, and making sure there was always a pot of hot coffee on the cook stove. We worked in shifts so the men who were searching could get a hearty meal anytime of the day or night.

We were ready to care for any cuts and scrapes, and we treated quite a few cases of frostbite. For several days following the storm, it turned bitterly cold. The wind died down but the temperatures plummeted, especially after sundown.

A few of the women pleaded with their husbands and sons to stop the search until it warmed up, but no one would listen. Perhaps they realized what no one would say. The frigid temperatures meant Pius wasn't wandering out there alone somewhere. What the men and boys were really searching for was his body. Still, one of our own had disappeared, and it didn't seem right that anyone should sleep until he was found. So the search continued.

On about the third day, Regina and I were assigned to work the afternoon shift together. Regina couldn't get control of herself. Every time someone walked through the door without Pius, she broke down crying. She kept telling everyone who came in that the love of her life was missing. She was so distraught that she couldn't help with the meals. In fact, she made it worse for those who stopped by for a bite to eat and a break from the bitterly cold search.

When she told me she had a sick headache and asked if I minded if she went home, I quickly nodded and helped her with her coat and cape. Because it was so cold, everyone wore as many layers as they could find. I nearly pushed her out the door, I was so relieved to be alone.

I'd been sitting there no more than an hour when the door opened and in walked Kermit. The circles under his eyes were so dark and deep I thought at first they were bruises. The skin on his face was red and chapped, and his lips were cracked. He probably hadn't slept in days. I pulled a chair out and pushed him into it with one hand as I poured him some coffee with the other. I set out a biscuit and jam and started to pull some meat from the chicken I'd just boiled for soup broth.

Kermit said, "Stop it, Ray. I don't deserve it. I need you to stop. Please, Ray. Can you just sit? I need to tell someone, and you're the only one I can trust. I can trust you, can't I?"

I sat. I nodded. Of course, he could trust me. If things had been different, I would have been his sister. Plus, he knew I wasn't going to tell anyone whatever he told me. I sensed an urgency in him. A sort of desperation, even. I knew the best way for me to help him was just to sit and listen as he'd asked me to.

As Kermit spoke in a monotone voice, his coffee grew cold in the untouched mug. "I'm responsible for Pius' disappearance. You see, I get these spells. I don't really know what comes over me, but my mind starts to race in such a bad way. I start thinking I'm unlovable. That I don't deserve happiness. That I will be left alone because I'm not worthy of love.

"I was the one who burned that church down back home, not Nicklaus. I didn't mean to. When I found out Nicklaus was leaving the next day and wasn't going to take me with him, I fell under a sort of haze. I got mad at him, but I was even angrier at myself because I wasn't worth anything to him. I started the fire in the church. I meant to burn myself up with it. And punish Nicklaus for not loving me more.

"The fire spread so quickly that my chest soon seized from the smoke. I must have fallen unconscious because the next thing I remember, I was outside with Nicklaus kneeling over me. He was shaking me and screaming my name. So he must have run into the church and dragged me out. He saved my miserable life."

Kermit buried his head in his hands. After a minute or so, he looked up and continued. "When I realized that Nicklaus had taken the blame before he left, I felt even worse. I spent many days alone thinking about what I'd done. I vowed to never let myself fall victim to that haze again.

"I set my eyes on America and began to work as hard as I could to make it here. I wanted to tell Nicklaus in person how much I loved him and how grateful I was to him for taking the blame for the evil I'd done. He gave me a future even as he tarnished his own. He was so unselfish. Such a great man! I came to realize that he truly did love me—with a love stronger than anything I'd ever known."

Tears stung my eyes, but Kermit's expression remained stony. I found it so strange that he could deliver such an emotional speech in such a flat tone of voice.

He went on. "When I heard Nicklaus had drowned. I grieved heavily. I didn't know what I had to live for. How would I go on? Why would I go on? Finally, I decided I'd come to America as planned and make a final resting place for myself next to Nicklaus.

"I didn't have a plan on how exactly to end my life, but I dreamed of that peaceful sleep. That sleep that would take me away from my impure thoughts and this blasted haze that never truly leaves me. It follows me. It plagues me. I am not a good person. Something inside of me pushes me to evil thoughts, and no matter how hard I try to fight it, my mind just won't rest.

"Well, I finally got on the boat to America, and that's where I met Pius. Suddenly, I had hope. I felt like maybe I could have a life. Maybe I could keep this haze in the background. He seemed to help me fight it. He made me *want* to fight it.

"Things were pretty good once we settled in this house. Then Regina started pestering us. I was so mad at Pius. I could see that if he didn't fall in love with Regina, it would be someone else. He's so talented. I mean, look at all this furniture. He *made* this with his own hands. He's just an incredible person. I knew things would change, and he'd leave for his own place. He'd forget me. And I'd be alone.

"I was mean to him. The haze came back, and I said terrible things. I told him to go sleep in his furniture shed. He did.

"And now he's gone."

Kermit grew very still. He sat in the chair that Pius had made. He rested his head in the crux of his arms on the table that Pius had polished to such brilliance. At last he sobbed. I placed my hand on his shoulder and allowed him to cry without interruption.

We stayed like this for at least half an hour. His sobs slowed, then stopped as he fell asleep. He slept soundly at the table even as several men came and went. A few suggested moving him to the bed, but I shook my head. Let him sleep, I thought. And he did. He slept for at least four hours. Maybe it was even more. I don't really know because Mrs. Kasper Schmidt came for her shift and sent me home.

They finally found Pius after three weeks of searching. When the snows began to thaw at the end of February, someone found his body in a dwindling snowbank about a mile from the house beside the railroad tracks. He'd been hit by the train.

We think he left his furniture shed and got turned around in the blizzard. He must have found the railroad track and decided to follow it into town. He likely thought he could take refuge at Noreen's until the wind let up. With the wind howling, he probably didn't even hear the train coming, and with the poor visibility, the engineer probably didn't even know he'd hit him. We all took the news hard.

Because it was winter and the ground was frozen, his remains were kept in his furniture shed until he could be buried. The townspeople gathered around Kermit and did their best to help him through. They knew that the two men had been as close as brothers, so they didn't think it strange that he took it so hard. Only I knew that he blamed himself.

After the funeral, Kermit came to me and asked me to write a letter to Pius' parents.

I tried to resist, but Kermit pleaded with me.

"Ray, you're so good with words. You knew him almost as well as I did, and I know you loved him, too. His parents deserve to know the kind of man he was, and I'm no good at things like that. Please, Ray. Those people raised a wonderful person, and they need to have a beautiful letter to remember him by."

I couldn't say no to him. He seemed so desperate. But the task came as a very heavy and unexpected burden. I didn't know what to write or how to start. I thought of little else for at least two weeks. Then at church one Sunday I heard the words Pius sang so often. Truth be told, I never knew they came from the Bible, but when I heard the pastor say them in church that day, I knew how to start my letter.

Dear Herr Und Frau Kornder,

"This is the day that the Lord hath made; I will rejoice and be glad in it." I heard your son, Pius, sing these words often. He was my friend, and I thought of him as a brother. Pius used to live in the loft above the barn of the family I live with. He sang these words loudly each morning. We could hear them from the house as we were getting breakfast started. He would sing them softly as I gathered his supper dishes and headed to the house in the evening. I even heard him sing them while he was making his beautiful furniture. These words bring me comfort, and I hope they will do the same for you.

You see, I am writing with very tragic news. Pius was on his way to town one day when the wind started to howl. It was so fierce it whipped the snow around and caused a complete white-out. It blinded him. He was lost in the storm and sought the railroad tracks as a way point. The wind was so loud there was no way for him to hear the train that took his life.

I wish with all my heart I didn't need to write you these words. Pius came to our community just two years ago, but he was instantly loved by everyone who met him. His sparkling hazel eyes will not be forgotten in these parts, that I can tell you.

I know that he loved each of you very much as well. I recall him talking about how much he missed his ma's biscuits. "Light as air and heavy with flavor," he would say.

No matter how much someone would compliment him on a piece of furniture he had just made, he would always shake his head and remark, "You should see the things my pa can make. On my best day I will never make anything as beautiful as he made on his worst."

Anytime he would see a baby girl with curly hair and blue eyes, he would get a bit misty and sigh, "Oh, but that little one does make me miss my little sis something terrible."

Pius was a good man and will be missed by so many. None more than his dear friend, Kermit. Kermit asked me to write you this letter. He told me that the people who raised such a beautiful human being deserved to know what a kind and gentle soul he was. He said that you should be very proud of him, and I agree.

If I close my eyes in the quiet of the night, I almost believe I can hear him singing from the heavens, "This is the day the Lord hath made; I will rejoice and be glad in it."

With loving memories of your dear son,
Shadow

That horrible winter turned to spring, and spring to summer. The seasons changed, and life on the prairie continued.

There was little time to grieve. As the snow melted, exposing the earth once again, thoughts turned to planting. If you want your family to survive, distractions like grief are a luxury you cannot afford.

Kermit was always a bit reclusive, but after Pius's death, he became even more so. He was rarely seen at church, and if he did attend, he sat in the back and left as soon as the sermon was over. Occasionally, he'd stop in town for supplies, but even then he tried not to talk with anyone. Often townsfolk saw him walking alone at sunset along the railroad tracks.

When I think back, it seems strange that the townsfolk didn't do more to help Kermit get through his grief—as they did with so many others. But then, Kermit didn't make it easy to do nice things for him. He rarely showed any appreciation, and he was just plain uncomfortable to be around. Mrs. Kasper Schmidt had called it an odd manner, and I guess that's as good a description as any. And even though Pius was a close friend, it wasn't like he was a member of anyone's family. Loss was commonplace, and grief was a part of life.

During this time, Kermit was short-tempered. One afternoon I saw him in town about a block down on the other side of the street walking the other way. I picked up my pace so I could greet him. I guessed we were both headed to the mercantile. The shopkeeper's dog had just given birth to a litter of puppies, and I was excited to see them. I have such a weakness for dogs. As I drew nearer, one of the pups ran out and tried to bite Kermit's boot. It was a playful gesture. But instead of tussling with the little dog or even walking by, he kicked it hard and sent it flying back into the shop with a yelp.

The shopkeeper came out and yelled at Kermit, but he just continued walking as if he didn't hear him. The puppy recovered, but everyone who saw the incident, including me, kept a distance from Kermit after that.

One day, as the autumn air was turning crisp and the crops had all been brought in for the winter to come, I was out in the coop collecting eggs. Suddenly, a gust of wind blew through the coop and gave me quite a shiver. An uneasy feeling came over me, and when I looked up, I saw Kermit standing there. He gave me quite a start. I hadn't seen him in weeks, and I sure wasn't expecting him to be in the chicken coop with me.

"Ray, I need to talk to you. Sorry I scared you, but I need to talk to you alone. Can you come for a walk?"

I looked around and saw no one. Hulda would not like me to go off with Kermit unchaperoned, but he seemed so desperate that I nodded and set the basket down. He led me over a little rise in the prairie where we couldn't be seen from the house. I tried to position myself to see him, but it was warmer if I kept the chill wind at my back, so we sat in the grass both looking toward the distance, facing the same direction.

"Ray, I've been doing a lot of thinking since Pius died. I don't belong here. I don't think I belong anywhere, really, but I know for dang sure it isn't here. I had a dream the other night. I was flying. I was looking over the town and all of the farms. Everyone was happy. I called to them from the air, but they didn't see me. That's how I feel. Like no one can see me.

"I'm leaving. I don't know when, but it'll be soon. I wanted to say good-bye to you. You're my only friend here. Or maybe anywhere," he mumbled, "and I want you to know I would have been proud for you to be my sister. If things had been different, Nicklaus would have been here to tell me what to do. But things aren't different, and they'll never change."

His words were filled with so much pain that tears were welling in my eyes as he spoke. I turned to look at him and touched his arm. He shrugged my hand off angrily. With completely dry eyes, he said, "No, I didn't come here for sympathy. I came to say good-bye. So, good-bye."

He got up and walked away.

I went back to finish collecting the eggs, but I felt very unsettled. I went over what he said in my mind a thousand times. Where would he go, and when would he leave? I thought about him wandering up and down the railroad tracks all those times and wondered if he'd been thinking about his next destination.

About a month or so later, it turned colder. A little snow had fallen, and as the sun set, the sky turned a deep orange. I knew that meant the wind would blow the next day. And it did. It blew hard enough to keep us indoors, only doing the most necessary of chores outside.

Once again, David arrived at Hulda and Herman's place just after breakfast with the news. Kermit had been found by the railroad tracks the day after the windstorm by some youngsters on their way to school. He'd been hit by the train and lay in an almost unrecognizable heap in the ditch beside the tracks.

It seemed everyone's first thought was for the children who found his body. They brought food to their homes and sat with their parents into the night discussing the traumatic discovery. There was a special service at church so we could all lay our hands on the youngsters and pray for them to cope with the memory of finding Kermit's mangled body.

I felt as if I was betraying my friend. No one seemed to think about him. No one discussed Kermit and the trauma he'd been dealing with. He had no family except the Kasper Schmidts to mourn him here, but it still felt wrong to completely dismiss his death.

I guess it was understandable, though. With the way Kermit had separated himself from the town, no one would miss him. No one but me.

All I could think about was that last strange conversation we shared outside the chicken coop that day. Had he been trying to tell me something? How had he not seen the train? Could I have done something? But what? I feared deep in my soul that he had chosen this particular death, but I didn't want to believe it.

About a week later, we received a visit from Cousin Kasper Schmidt. He and his wife had gone to Kermit's place to collect his things and get the homestead ready to sell off. When they arrived, they saw Pius's furniture shed burned to the ground. Nothing but a few tools could be salvaged.

When they entered the house, they found it very clean and tidy. Everything was in its place, and on the table was a piece of paper, folded neatly in half. Cousin Kasper handed Herman the letter. I immediately recognized it as the same parchment that Pius had purchased when he asked me to write those letters for him. That seemed like such a long time ago. "How could it have only been three years past?" I thought.

Herman stood by his guest near the door and read the letter aloud. I was on my corner stool by the cook stove. Hulda sat at the table while Regina washed the dishes. The boys were outside doing chores.

The letter was short. It said,

I need to leave. I have no one here now who cares for me but Ray. I want her to have the house, the land, and all my belongings. She is really my only family here. Or as close to family as I have known since my sweet Pius left me alone.

Yours,

Kermit Haberer

P.S. You know Ray as Shadow.

I was overwhelmed with emotion. So many feelings rushed at me all at once. Even now, I can't find the words to describe how heavy my heart was as Herman read those words.

As you can imagine, news of the letter caused quite a stir. There was a lot of discussion that day and in the days that followed about me and my relationship with Kermit and Pius. Gossip and rumors were flying. Hulda took to bed with a sick headache and said she wasn't sure she could ever show her face again.

You can't keep Hulda down for long, though. Once she had a chance to think about it, she knew I hadn't done anything to be ashamed of. She decided to set everyone straight by reminding them that I had been Kermit's brother's sweetheart. That was all there was to it.

Regina became angry with me. She accused me of trying to take one of the only eligible bachelors worth having on the entire prairie. She stopped talking to me and tried as hard as she could not to be in the same room with me. I didn't understand that at all. Regina had eyes for Pius, not for Kermit. She seldom glanced in his direction. After Pius died, her excuses to visit that house disappeared. And, as I have said, Kermit made it difficult to be friendly with him. Regina kept her distance just like the rest of us. But after Regina found out that Kermit had given me his house, she seemed to imagine a past that had never existed.

I tried not to pay attention. I couldn't concentrate on any of the drama that surrounded me. My worst fears had been confirmed. When Kermit said good-bye to me that day, he was saying good-bye to more than the town, more than to me. He was saying farewell to everything. To his very *life!* I saw it all so clearly then, but what could I have done to save him? The question haunts me to this day.

When the wind blows, I'm always reminded of Kermit. It calls to me. Asking me to do something. Anything. Pleading with me to make the howling stop. But this wind never gives me answers. It never tells me what I should have done. What I could have done. What I should do now. There is no peace in the wind.

That's how I came to live in this house. My Nicklaus had wanted it for me to live in with him. Now I live here with only his memory to keep me company. I do love the place. I feel comforted knowing and having loved the one who designed it, the one who built it, and the one who furnished it.

This house is mine. Yes, I own the property. But it's more than that. This house is part of my soul. It's part of who I am, who I was, and who I could have been. I find peace here. I find rest in this place.

But tonight all I can think about is this wind. I feel restless. This wind makes me nervous.

Regina

Regina was the closest thing to a sister I have ever known. When I think of her, and I do so often, it's always with a tender smile in my heart. Hulda gave birth to her when I was about six or seven.

Oh, I wish I could tell you my exact age, but as I've explained, I don't know when I was born. The date of my birth has been a mystery to me my whole life. I remember watching the other children on their birthdays as they opened little gifts and ate the sweets made in their honor while everyone sang to them. I was never jealous of the focused attention, but I did think it would be lovely to have a special day just for me. But enough of my fussing; this story is about Regina, not about silly birthdays or the lack of them.

From birth, Regina was a fetching little thing with blonde hair and blue eyes. Her eyelashes were so thick and long that when she batted them at you, her eyes seemed to dance. Regina learned to use those dancing eyes to her advantage almost from the moment she was born. It seemed to me that people would do just about anything to make her smile so they could watch that sweet little face light up with joy. And she was a happy little thing. Hardly ever a cry or whine came out of her mouth. As she grew older, she added a shy little giggle to the flash of her eyes, and no one could resist her charms.

Being Hulda and Herman's only daughter, she was the apple of her daddy's eye, and her mother doted on her like no one else. Regina brought out a side of Hulda I'd never seen. With Regina, she was patient and restrained. She'd sit for hours with Regina on her lap, talking sweetly to her. Hulda took great pride in fixing her hair and making her pretty little outfits to wear on Sundays. I'd say Regina was a spoiled child, but that would imply she was naughty. She wasn't disobedient; she just knew how to manipulate any situation to her favor.

It's hard to describe the closeness I felt for her. As I said, she was almost like a sister to me. I felt proud when the other women fussed over her at church. The older ladies loved to hold her on their laps, singing songs to her that made her giggle. Sometimes they played patty cake with her or fussed with the ribbons Hulda always decorated her hair with. Truly, she was so pampered that she was nearly two before she walked! I liked watching Hulda's face swell with pride as she accepted the compliments that always showered her sweet baby girl.

I was often left to watch over Regina while Hulda did her chores and worked in the kitchen to keep the boys fed. She was an easy child to look after most of the time. Regina loved to be outdoors and would sit for hours watching the birds fly by or playing with a worm in the dirt. She found such wonder and beauty in nature.

Once when we were much older, Regina and I were sitting on the little hill on the west side of the barn. We were watching the sunset in the quiet of the late summer evening. Regina bent over and whispered to me, "Shadow, would you look at that sky! How could anyone not believe there is a God when you see something so beautiful right in your own back yard?"

I usually enjoyed my time alone with her when she was a toddler. But I have to admit, sometimes I felt her presence an unnecessary burden as I tried to get my own work done.

One day when she was about three years old, I was finishing up the breakfast dishes and getting ready to peel some potatoes for the men's dinner. I only turned my back for a moment when I found Regina lying on the floor of the kitchen, rolling this way and that. She was making shallow gasping sounds. Her lips were starting to turn blue, and her eyes were wide open and searching. I was so frightened. I ran to her and shook her a little. I didn't know what was happening, but I knew something was desperately wrong.

I scurried outside to where Hulda was hanging laundry and tugged at her skirt.

"Shoo away! Can't you see I'm busy?" she scolded.

I didn't give up. I kept tugging at her until she had no choice but to follow me into the house. She saw little Regina right away and started screaming for Herman. I ran outside to find him, but he'd already heard Hulda and was running to the house from the barn.

He flew into the kitchen. When he saw Regina, his face lost all its color. "I'm hitchin' up the horses. We got to get her into town to the doc right away!"

With a determined look on her face, Hulda scooped Regina, now limp and silent, into her arms and started running after Herman toward the barn. She was in such a hurry that she stumbled on a rock and fell face first into the dirt right on top of Regina.

Herman yelled, "For the love of God, woman, watch yourself. You'll kill her for sure!"

Hulda let out an ear-splitting, high pitched wail. I stopped dead in my tracks in the yard as I watched Hulda roll off the toddler and move to pick her little body back up. Hulda rarely showed emotion, but I could see the tears in her eyes as I started running toward them.

Then a miracle happened. We heard these windy, gasping sounds coming from Regina as she started to take deeper and deeper breaths. Herman stopped his work with the horses and stared at Hulda and the child. They both started crying right along with Regina. I cried, too. The crisis was past. She had turned a corner, and the episode—whatever it was that had overcome her— was at an end.

The two frightened parents discussed it and decided it was best to take her into town to see the doctor to make sure their cherished little daughter would survive. Without being asked, I climbed into the wagon and sat in the open space behind the bench where Hulda and Regina sat. I'm not certain they even knew I was there, but I sure didn't want to be left behind. I wanted to know what the doctor would say.

By the time Herman had the horses hitched and we were settled in the wagon, Regina had regained all of her color and was giggling at a ladybug that had landed on her dress. When we got to town, the doctor performed a brief examination and listened as the nervous parents told him the details. He said Regina had probably been chocking on something, and when Hulda fell on her, the force was enough to dislodge the obstruction.

Hulda, who had been clenching her fists and sitting on the edge of her seat this whole time, slumped back into the stiff-backed chair. "Humph. I guess I saved her life," she mumbled, almost to herself.

If Hulda doted on her before, I don't know what you'd call her attention toward her daughter after that. It was as if Regina were made out of porcelain. Both parents watched and petted her to such a degree that it caused a bit of gossip around town.

After Hulda and Regina walked away, ladies would whisper, "That little one is going to get herself into trouble if there isn't discipline in the home." And, more than once I heard, "Children need to be given a bit of freedom once in a while to learn right from wrong on their own." And, my favorite: "A little dirt never hurt anyone."

Being the only two girls in the house, Regina and I spent many hours together doing chores for Hulda. While the men were in the fields, we were cleaning, milking, gardening, and doing all the other things one must do to keep a house running efficiently on the prairie.

Hulda gave us a list of tasks to accomplish each day, and we'd set to work as soon as the breakfast dishes were washed. Keeping Regina on task was never a small undertaking. She was so easily distracted. We'd be pulling weeds in the vegetable garden, and I'd look her way to see how much progress she was making only to find her trying to get a butterfly to land on a little stick. Or she'd be lying flat on her back next to the garden looking at the clouds. She could do that for hours. Regina had such an imagination. Sometimes she'd invent whole villages, complete with castles, dragons, and princesses moving in the sky above us.

As much as I was annoyed at having to do more than my share of the work, I loved hearing the stories she told. Sometimes when I looked up, I could actually see the shape of the man on the horse with a sword or the herd of buffalo she was describing. I heard someone say, "That little Regina walks around with her head in the clouds most of the time." I thought to myself, "If they only knew the half of it."

Right before Regina's eleventh birthday, she and I were walking to town to get some sugar and flour for the cakes Hulda was planning to make in honor of the day. Hulda always made two or three of her famous white frosted cakes for Regina's birthday. Her cakes were the best in town, and I know more than one who marked their calendars to stop by for a visit on Regina's birthday just to be offered a slice. Her birthdays were always marked by visitors from all over the township.

On the way to the mercantile, Regina sighed heavily and said, "Oh, Shadow, I'm so bored. Nothing ever *happens* here. It is just the same thing one day to the next."

I think about that simple comment sometimes, even now. How often have I heard someone wish for something to happen? It seems to me that when you're wishing for something different to happen, you're missing the things that are occurring all around you every second.

I've never understood this sense of restlessness. How could Regina think nothing ever happens? The seasons change the way the whole landscape looks. The weather changes from wind, to rain, to sun, to snow. There is always work to be done, a funeral to plan, a garden to tend, or a new mother to visit. You truly never know what will happen from the time you wake up in the morning to the time you lay your head back on your pillow. Regina, like so many others, seemed to always be wishing for something else instead of appreciating what was so clearly already there.

I remember the exact day this conversation occurred because of what happened the next day. The day of Regina's eleventh birthday, we met Siegfried Malsom and his wife Johanna. The young couple had just settled on the old Otto place on the edge of town. Mr. Otto, an old bachelor, had passed the year before, and his place had sat empty until the Malsoms took it over.

I think I must have been about seventeen or so. I hadn't met Nicklaus yet. Ah, my sweet Nicklaus. I seem to mark time as "before Nicklaus," "during Nicklaus," and "after Nicklaus." I miss him so much sometimes. But here I go fussing again. Let me get back to the story.

Siegfried and Johanna had come for cake with the neighbors. The minute Regina saw Johanna, she took to her. Johanna looked young for her age. She was almost thirty years old with light brown hair and dark brown eyes. She wore her hair in a high bun on top of her head with a ring of little flowers around it. Her dress was of the latest style, and she wore high heeled shoes with leather adornments on the toes and sides. She was so fashionable. Really, we had never seen anyone like her on the prairie.

Siegfried was also striking. He was very handsome with a big, long mustache that curled at the tips. He had a white shirt with a little ruffle around the buttons and black high-waisted pants. You could see right away that Siegfried was older than his wife. He was almost 40. In those days a big age difference between man and wife wasn't unusual. Couples just found each other without regard for the number of years that separated them.

Siegfried brought his family to the area to set up a newspaper. It was something everyone was very excited about. Even those who couldn't read were delighted at the prospect of regular news updates, and a few even started taking lessons from the schoolmarm on Sunday afternoons.

As soon as they walked in the door, Regina's eyes flew open wide and a smile appeared on her face. She ran up to Johanna and put her arm through hers. Regina looked up into the newcomer's eyes and said, "I think we're going to be best friends." And so it was.

Even though there was an age difference of nineteen years between the two, it didn't seem to matter to either. They were almost inseparable. I think Johanna was lonesome for a friend as she became acquainted with prairie life. For Regina's part, she'd found someone who could show her another possibility for her life. Even at her young age, Regina had a hunger to leave the slow pace of country life and explore the wonders of a city.

Johanna grew up in New York as the daughter of a newspaper man, so she was sophisticated and cultured. She moved gracefully and sat with her hands perfectly folded. Instead of churning butter, she played the piano. (They actually brought a piano all the way from the East.) Instead of darning socks, she spent her days perfecting her embroidery stitches. I still have one of the handkerchiefs she made.

Truth be told, I didn't care much for Johanna. She was pampered and spent too much time complaining about small town life. Many times I heard her call folks dull and uneducated.

It is true that people in these parts didn't have fancy balls or eat expensive foods prepared by others. It is also true that most everyone could barely read or write, and many in these parts had only an eighth grade education. Still, the people here have always had big and generous hearts. They're hardworking and God-fearing people. I didn't like the way she was always acting like she was better than the rest of them.

None of that bothered Regina, though. In fact, she picked up on Johanna's superior attitude and started to complain herself. I tried to spend as little time with the two of them as I could. But their friendship did work to my advantage sometimes.

A few months after Siegfried Malsom set up the newspaper, I met my Nicklaus. I sometimes led Hulda to believe that I was going to tag along with Regina to visit Johanna, but instead I'd sneak off to meet my Nicklaus. Regina was often in town keeping Johanna company while Siegfried worked long hours at his newspaper office. That gave me plenty of freedom to come and go as my relationship with Nicklaus blossomed.

Johanna and Siegfried had two little girls, ages six and ten, with a third on the way that spring day when they arrived for cake to celebrate Regina's birthday. Regina grew to love those girls and watched over the two giggling things like a favorite aunt. She was always bringing them flowers from the garden or showing them how to make things like straw dolls. They, of course, preferred to play with the paper dolls they had brought from the East, but that didn't stop Regina from bringing them little gifts.

Even though Regina was so close in age to Johanna's daughter, she seemed so much older. Life in the country makes one more disciplined than life in a city. One needs to learn quickly and develop a keen common sense. The Malsom girls may have been cultured but they didn't possess the maturity that Regina did.

Regina said to me, "Shadow, those girls have the most darling names. They are named after flowers! Rose is the oldest, Daisy is next, and Johanna said she plans to name the baby Marigold if it's another girl. Johanna hopes the baby is a girl. She said Siegfried is hoping for a boy. He wants a son, but she thinks having sons is so expected. Of course, a man would want a son, but to raise only girls, that would be really something, wouldn't it?"

The baby was a girl, and they did name her Marigold.

Regina didn't speak much about Siegfried. When she did, it was usually in passing and with a tone of tolerance. I felt that Regina put up with Siegfried because she wouldn't be able to spend time with Johanna unless he was always working. For his part, he seemed happy that his little wife had found a companion and was starting to adjust to small town life on the prairie.

Siegfried was born in the old country and came to America just a few years before they moved to Dakota. He'd been studying English back home and was quite a good writer. He met Johanna in New York when she was working as a typesetter at her father's newspaper office. She said that her father was trying to "teach her the value of a hard day's work" and insisted she go to the office with him every morning. Her father hired Siegfried as a reporter.

Johanna said that she often had to call the newcomer down to typesetting to help her make sense of his poor handwriting. Before long, they fell in love and got married. They decided to move west where Siegfried could, with the help of a sizable loan from his father-in-law, pursue his dream of starting his own newspaper.

I'm not clear now on exactly why they chose our little town to settle in. Neither of them knew anyone here as far as I can remember. Maybe like many others in those days, they went as far as they could until they just got too tired to keep going. They arrived by train, and after a brief respite at Noreen's place, they bought the Otto homestead and Siegfried got to work.

Johanna and Regina spent as much time together as possible, which was quite a lot actually. With Siegfried working long hours trying to get his newspaper started, Johanna was idle much of the time. Hulda demanded Regina do her chores, but once they were completed, she was released to pursue her own interests. Regina would often come home from her visits with Johanna and tell Hulda how useless Johanna was in home keeping. She thought Johanna was so refined she had no need to know the basics of keeping a house in order.

Regina gleefully said that Johanna was teaching her to be a lady, and she was trying to teach Johanna enough to get by as a country woman. Hulda would huff a bit during these accounts. But Regina would remind her that the prairie is much different than the city and that Johanna needed time to learn.

As you can imagine, there was a great deal of talk around town when Johanna posted a flyer at Noreen's asking for live-in help. The flyer said she needed help caring for her two (soon to be three) small children, the cooking and cleaning, as well as the other household chores.

Hulda definitely had her opinions on the matter. "I have never heard of such a thing in my life!" Hulda stated one night over supper. "That woman has two little girls who she should be teaching to clean and help with the meals instead of lazing around with nothing of value to do like their mother. What does she do all day if she isn't taking care of her own children? That poor man is working all day at his newspaper, and instead of coming home to a hot meal and well-behaved children, he has to fend for himself!

"Regina says she doesn't even know how to make an apple crisp. Can you believe that? Regina had to show her how to make a crisp! She wanted a recipe, and Regina had to tell her there is no need for a recipe when you're just making a crisp. Now she wants live-in help? I have seen everything!"

This went on for a while until Herman said, "Enough, Hulda. Let Siegfried handle his wife. You don't need to get so heated. This doesn't concern you."

Hulda kept quiet that night, but she and the other women had plenty more to say at the church circle the following week. The group gossiped so much that they hardly made any progress on the quilt they were making for the new pastor.

Of course, it all stopped when Mrs. Bietelspracher applied for the job. Her husband, Mr. Bietelspracher, had been kicked in the head by their cow a few months back. They found him in the barn, and he immediately had trouble walking and couldn't remember things that had just happened. His wife got him to bed and cared for him the best she could, but he only lived a few days after the accident.

The doctor, who'd been out of town when it happened, said loudly at the funeral luncheon, "The trauma to the head obviously caused his brain to swell, so he should have been kept upright and awake. Putting him to bed is likely what killed the poor man!"

This declaration caused Mrs. Bietelspracher to wail with grief, sorrow, and guilt. Hulda overheard the comment and quickly gave the doctor a good dressing down. "Why would you tell a poor grieving widow something like that? Have you no soul? Where is your heart, your compassion?"

The doctor squared his shoulders at the assault and replied, "I have an obligation to instruct others so as to prevent future unnecessary deaths like this. I will not apologize or be accused of wrongdoing by the medically uneducated!"

Hulda turned red, and her eyes bulged. Thankfully, Herman was there to gently but firmly guide his wife to the wagon, saying, "I think we best be headin' for home now."

We all thought that one of the two Bietelspracher boys would come home and take over the farm after their father's death, but neither one did. The older son had gone out West in search of gold in the Black Hills. Word was that he'd fallen into bad company out in Deadwood and turned his back on his upbringing.

The younger moved out East and married the daughter of a successful businessman. He chose to stay with his wife's family instead of coming back to the family farm. You'd think this would have broken Mrs. Bietelspracher's heart, but she was a strong woman and said she would play the cards the good Lord saw fit to deal her.

So when word got out that the Malsoms were hiring live-in help, Mrs. Bietelspracher saw it as a sign from God. She put the farm up for sale, moved to town, and lived in the back room of the Malsom place.

Johanna was very relieved to have such a capable woman taking care of her and her little family. And the town gossip died away as the women saw what a blessing the situation was for everyone involved.

Over the next year or so, things seemed to go well for the Malsom family. Mrs. Bietelspracher proved to be a wonderful cook and an efficient and tidy housekeeper. The newspaper's circulation grew. Johanna spent her days teaching her two older daughters and Regina about the finer things in life while Mrs. Bietelspracher cared for the baby.

Johanna taught the girls to draw and play the piano while bringing their voices in tune with the keys. The younger girls watched as Johanna taught Regina how to put ribbons in her hair in keeping with the latest fashion and how to powder her face with rice flour and to brighten her lips and cheeks with crushed flower petals.

One afternoon while she watched me weed the garden, Regina told me that because of Johanna's instruction, the boys were starting to take notice of her. Regina loved to be the center of attention, and Johanna taught her to use her developing femininity to attract the eyes and gentlemanly gestures of many of the young men in town.

Regina laughed as she told me how she could get them to do almost anything for her she wished. Of course, the boys would open doors for her and offer to carry her books or purchases from the mercantile. But what she found most amusing was that she could also get them to buy her little sweets or even put their jackets over a puddle so she could walk without getting her shoes wet.

Regina met Johanna on her eleventh birthday, and by the time she turned twelve, Regina was developing into a beautiful young woman. And, under Johanna's tutelage, she was demanding to be treated like a pampered one.

Regina and Hulda rarely bickered because Hulda generally gave Regina whatever she wanted, but there were often arguments about the face powder and rouge Regina insisted on wearing every chance she got. Hulda put her foot down on Sundays, though. She said, "The Lord has no use for vanity. On His day, you will refrain from covering the natural beauty He gave you with such nonsense."

A little over a year after the Malsoms arrived in town, our little village was visited by the Blue Death epidemic. We now call this disease cholera, but back then, it was only referred to as the Blue Death.

It was all anyone could talk about, and people tried to do all sorts of things to stop the spread. Some shoved rugs under the door cracks. Others wouldn't leave the house even for church. At the same time, some started sleeping outdoors, claiming they needed fresh air in their lungs to fend off the illness.

As the outbreak spread, Mrs. Bietelspracher's younger son coincidentally wrote to his mother that he and his wife would like her to move to their home in the East. He said that if she was to take care of someone's house and children, he would like her to take care of his.

Mrs. Bietelspracher didn't take long to consider the move. Within a week of the letter, she packed her belongings yet again and boarded the train.

On the Sunday afternoon before she left, she told Hulda over coffee and cake, "I love those little girls and will miss all of you on the prairie, but my heart aches to see my own flesh and blood. I can't wait to hold my boy in my arms again and to meet his wife and my grandbabies!"

With Mrs. Bietelspracher gone, Johanna and Siegfried were left to face the Blue Death by themselves. The baby wasn't quite two years old yet, and Johanna was struggling to care for the three little girls by herself. She had never been interested in keeping house, and now her lack of knowledge overwhelmed her. To make matters worse, Hulda refused to let Regina leave the farm. She said she didn't want Regina to catch her death by gallivanting around needlessly, and that was all there was to it.

Siegfried spent even more time at the office because several of his employees had either fallen ill or were home taking care of family members who had.

The disease came on quickly and violently. Diarrhea and vomiting caused the stricken to shrivel up and turn a bluish gray color before their eventual death. While some survived, most died within five to twelve days of the first sign of sickness. Sadly, the doctor was among the first to be taken, which left the rest of the town to fend for themselves.

Regina was sick with worry for her friend and the sweet little girls she'd come to love so dearly. Finally, Hulda relented a bit. She told Regina that she would send me to the Malsom place with a basket of preserves, bread, and soup. Regina spent the better part of a day drawing little pictures for the girls and writing notes to Johanna.

With the basket on my arm, I set off for town. I had walked that way so many times before that I could have made the journey with my eyes closed. But this time it was different. At every step, I was sure the Blue Death was going to jump out and attack me. None of us knew how it was being spread so quickly. I imagined the sickness was hiding under the rocks or behind the trees, just waiting to attach itself to an unsuspecting victim.

I admit I cried that day on my way to town. I didn't want to die that way. But I knew if someone were to be sacrificed, it made sense it would be me. So I continued on, praying and watching as I moved down the familiar path.

When I arrived at the Malsom place with the basket, I discovered Johanna in an alarming state. Her hair looked as if it hadn't been combed for days, and her eyes were red and swollen from crying.

She was happy to see the basket, though. She quickly reached into it, pulled out each item, and read each note. She told me that the baby had become ill, and she just didn't know what to do. Siegfried was at his office, and she was left alone to fight this plaque by herself.

She wrote a quick note back to Regina, placed it in the basket, and I left. My heart broke for her, and yet I was so thrilled to be going back to the safety of the farm that I nearly ran out of the house.

It was terribly cold, and the wind was whipping up. That winter when the Blue Death was all around us was a bad one.

There was a blizzard coming, and I was all by myself. I was scared.

Then, suddenly, my Nicklaus appeared. He was heading home after helping the neighbors get their animals fed. Luck was on our side because our paths crossed just as we were passing the old Oskar place. We ducked inside and spent a wonderful few hours together.

As much as we enjoyed that day, Nicklaus said we couldn't risk doing so again until the Blue Death plague was over. He didn't want to risk passing the disease on to me.

Back at the farm, Regina read the note and discussed it with her mother. She and Hulda decided that I must return the next day with another basket. I did as I was told that day and the days that followed.

I won't write down the details of what I saw in the Malsom home on those subsequent visits. I think it best to leave that to your imagination. I will say, though, that it was horrifying. Each day I brought a basket and each day I returned with an empty one.

Johanna had even stopped writing Regina the little notes. She was just too exhausted. Regina pressed me for information, but I don't talk, and I don't think I would have described what I saw even if I could have. The baby died within five days, and within a month, the two girls and their mother were gone as well.

When I arrived with the final basket, I found only Siegfried. He was slumped over his desk in the parlor. When he looked up at me, I could see the depth of his despair in the gaunt and lifeless eyes that reflected my pale and grief stricken mirror image.

I set the basket down on the floor and pulled the piano bench beside his chair. I didn't know what to do, so I just placed my hand on his shoulder. I wouldn't have known what to say even if I could have offered any words of comfort. All I could do was be silently present, a non-speaking witness to his heartache.

He shuddered beneath my touch. After several minutes in this position, he began to talk.

"Shadow, thank you for coming, and thank you for helping to care for my beautiful little angels. But your generosity doesn't change my belief that this town is an awful, evil place. I look around, and can't think of one good reason to have come here. Most of the people here can't read, or at least can't read well enough to understand my articles. Those that can seem to prefer gossip to news.

"Yes, I've managed to make a little bit of money, but we've been living mostly on my father-in-law's generosity. Without him wiring me the advances, we would have been ruined long ago.

"Now, this plague. This Blue Death has taken everything that ever meant anything to me. How am I going to tell this man that I've squandered his money on a lost cause and return without his daughter and granddaughters?

"Shadow, I had everything, and now I have nothing. I hate this place. Everywhere I look, every corner, I see nothing but failure and death.

"I'm leaving on the first train I can get and going back to the old country where none of this can follow me.

"Thank you for coming, but now please go, and leave me as you found me."

What could I do? I left and went back to the farm. No note this time. Only tears. Johanna may have been pampered, and I didn't like the way she talked about the townsfolk, but she did her best and was always so kind to Regina. The girls were eleven, seven, and almost two when they died. Too young by anyone's standard. When I arrived home, I went quickly to my quiet little stool by the stove and started mending socks. I couldn't look Regina, or anyone, in the eye that afternoon.

David stopped by after supper that night. He came to share the news of the death of the last Malsom girl followed only a day later by her mother. There were several other deaths to report as well, but it was the Malsoms who seemed to have suffered the greatest loss. David told Herman that Siegfried boarded the train and said he wouldn't be back.

We all turned to Regina. We felt she would be inconsolable with grief. But instead, she stared expressionless, straight ahead with her face to the wall. As tears fell from her eyes, she said in an oddly calm and steady voice, "It's up to me, then."

At the time I didn't understand what she meant. But the years that followed revealed what was on her mind. Regina tended the graves of her friend and the young girls with loving care until she left the prairie. She planted a rosebush, daisies, and marigolds beside the girls' graves. On Johanna's she planted three peony bushes, one deep fuchsia, one white, and one pink. She groomed the little flower garden with more attention, care, and dedication than I ever thought she was capable of.

I took up the chore of caring for those graves after she left. I wonder who will care for them when I'm gone. Who will even remember who they were?

The Blue Death arrived in the township in October, and by the end of February, it was gone. For the most part, it passed over Hulda and Herman's place. One of the boys fell ill, but Hulda forced so much chicken broth down him that the plague couldn't stick.

Theophil's family was spared completely, as was David's. Life began to return to its normal routine. The seasons come and the seasons go. One can't take too much time to dwell on the past when you have so much work to do.

In April that same year, Herbert Baum invited everyone to the picnic by the lake on his place. You may remember me telling you about that day. That is the day I lost my Nicklaus. It was a hard year for a lot of folks. Between the Blue Death and the drownings, too many good people were lost.

Regina was at the lake the day of the drownings. She had been so sad after her friend Johanna and the girls died. The face of the joy-filled girl who was always full of laughter was replaced by one of despair that often seemed on the verge of tears.

But that beautiful spring day, she seemed to have forgotten her grief for a time. I remember seeing her smile and giggle a little with her friends before Edith Schoenmann lost her false teeth and set off the horror that followed.

Regina was such a sensitive soul. I remember how she sat with me for several hours over the course of the weeks that followed. I think she knew how deeply I hurt inside. She usually chatted away without saying anything. Just filling the silence with her voice. But sometimes she told me how empty she felt. How the loss of life left her with a huge void within her soul. It helped me some to cope with my own grief to know that I wasn't alone. Regina, at least, felt the same way.

As you may also recall, the following year, Kermit and Pius came to town. Regina was head over heels for Pius and tried to get his attention at every turn. She employed every flirtatious technique that Johanna had taught her. She told me once, "Shadow, I know the others are talking about me, but when I'm with Pius and he smiles at me, I lose some of that emptiness. Once he held my hand for a moment when no one was looking. I swear, I felt whole again. I don't care! Let them all talk!"

After Pius was hit by the train, followed by Kermit the following winter, I moved into my little house. The house that my Nicklaus dreamed would one day be ours. I felt safe and comforted by the house, but I was lonesome. I had never lived alone before. I longed to be surrounded by the family again, and I hungered for company. But I didn't feel I belonged there anymore. Hulda and Herman raised me and gave me food and shelter as long as I needed it. But I didn't need their help any longer, and I couldn't continue to pester Hulda. So I sat in my little house with more idle time than I had ever known.

It was a welcome surprise when Regina showed up on my doorstep one sunny summer afternoon. I had just taken a loaf of bread from the oven, and it was still warm. So I sliced her a big piece and set the butter and jam on the table as I put on a kettle for coffee. I hoped she would stay a while.

As Regina sat at my table eating her fresh bread and drinking coffee, she told me that she had come to plead with me to return home. I was shocked by this request and sat at the table looking at her with confusion.

"Oh, Shadow, Ma has been as crunchy as ever since you left. She complains non-stop about the amount of work that has piled up since you're gone.

"This morning, Dad asked me to help him in the barn. I knew something was up because the barn is for the boys. I figured he wanted to talk to me about somethin' without being overheard. So I followed him.

"He said, 'Regina, you got to go get Shadow. Your ma is lookin' tired, and I can't take her complainin' anymore. She'd never ask herself, so someone has to do it for her. Go tell Shadow we need her. But don't breathe a word to your Ma or anyone else or we'll all get a whoopin'!'

"So, Shadow, that's why I'm here. Will you come back?"

My heart leapt as she spoke. I was shocked at how much joy I felt to know that I was needed. I was feeling lost and without purpose. Plus, I was learning that having too much time alone with only my own thoughts was not good for me. I'd found myself near tears on many occasions. Sometimes even in the middle of the day! Now, I was being asked to return.

I nodded that I would spend more time at the house and help Hulda. Regina suggested I come the following day so Hulda wouldn't suspect that she came to fetch me. It was a good plan.

I arrived the on schedule with a batch of cinnamon rolls. Hulda looked at me, took the rolls, and said, "Humph! I don't have time to put on a pot of coffee for you. I'm plumb wore out. If you want a cup, you're gonna have to make it yourself."

I put the coffee on, and while I waited for it to heat, I started washing the dishes from breakfast. Then I set out two cups and dished up a couple of the rolls. I motioned for Hulda to sit down at the table. To my surprise, she did as I urged without argument.

As we ate the pastry, she surprised me again when she said, "It's sure nice to see you, Shadow."

That settled it. From that morning on, I would get up early and make myself breakfast. Then I would walk to the farm and help Hulda and Regina with the housework. After the supper dishes were done, I'd walk back home.

The days were long, but I felt that my help was not only wanted but appreciated. God meant for us to share our lives in community with others. He blessed me with Hulda and Herman and their family. I was content to be there.

Regina, however, hadn't been able to overcome the grief she felt over the loss of Johanna and her girls, those lost in the drownings, and then Pius and Kermit. She seemed to carry the deaths in a very personal way. Regina fell into a very deep depression. When she was seventeen years old, I overheard Hulda tell Herman, "She's too young to be so hangdog. We need to do something. I miss my daughter. Truly, I'm worried about her. I think we should send her to the city to visit my cousin for a spell."

Herman must have thought it was a good idea because within a month, she was on a train with her small trunk headed to Minneapolis.

Before she left, Regina was thrilled about the prospect of seeing the city. She talked nonstop about what she imagined it would be like and what she would see and do. Johanna had filled her head with so many fanciful ideas that Regina couldn't wait to leave the prairie for this new and exciting adventure.

After Hulda waved good-bye to the train, she excused herself to the outhouse by the station. She was in there a long while, and as we stood on the platform waiting for her, we could hear the sobs. Hulda loved Regina so much and had never been apart from her before. I think it shows what a remarkably strong person Hulda was to sacrifice her own happiness to try to bring joy back to her daughter.

They got a short letter from Regina about a month later. She said she was having a wonderful time and had met many interesting people. She missed the prairie and her family, though, and was planning to return the following month. Hulda and Herman were glad to hear this, and Hulda started preparing the feast she would have in honor of Regina's return. You can be sure there was more than one of her famous white frosted cakes at that party.

The first thing I noticed when Regina got home was that her clothes fit tighter. She had gained weight in the city. She was even curvier than before, and it looked good on her. Jack teased, "By gosh, you're so fat I swear we sent one sister to the city and got two back." Regina said there wasn't much to do in the city so she mostly sat around and ate rich food.

She wasn't feeling well, though. She had trouble eating, especially in the mornings, and was very tired all of the time.

Within a couple of weeks, Hulda realized that her precious, unwed, seventeen-year-old daughter was expecting a baby.

In those days it was customary to send a girl in that situation away until after the birth. The baby would be given up for adoption, and with luck, no one would suspect a thing. The trouble here was that Regina had just returned home from a trip. Who would believe that she was just "going visiting" so soon after her return? But more importantly, Hulda couldn't bear to send Regina away again.

One morning, after the men went to the field and we were cleaning up the breakfast dishes, Hulda looked Regina square in the face. "You listen to me, little girl. I know you got yourself into trouble in that godforsaken city. I want you to tell me the name of the man that did this to you, and I'm going to demand he come and marry you."

Regina's face went pale. She said, "Ma, I'll never tell you or anyone else his name. He is in the past, and I don't ever plan to speak of him. Ever."

"Well, I'm not sending you away again. If you don't want to do the right thing and get married, you can just suffer the consequences of your actions. You will raise that child, and that's the end of it."

Regina ran to her bed and cried until she fell asleep and wouldn't get out of bed even for supper.

That night as the men gathered around the table, Hulda told Herman and the boys that Regina was going to have a baby. "Your sister won't say who the father is."

Jack's ten-year-old mouth fell open. "What do you mean she's going to have a baby? She's not even married. How can you have a baby unless you're married?"

Hulda shot him a look. "I don't need any of your sass today!"

Jack looked shocked. "But Ma, that wasn't sass. I don't understand what the heck is going on."

In a low voice, Herman responded, "Jack, I can explain this all to you some other time. It's possible to have a baby without a wedding, but it's a powerful shameful thing. I will say that much."

"Where is she, anyway?" Jack's eyes flashed in anger as this realization took shape in his mind.

"Your sister has taken to bed," Hulda replied. "I told her if she didn't tell us who did this to her so we could find him and make him do the right thing by her, she would have to suffer the consequences on her own. She's been up there for hours."

"But if she's gonna have a baby, her belly is gonna get big! People will know she doesn't have a husband. Ma, folks are gonna talk. What are we supposed to do? We can't fight everyone in town to keep them from talkin'!"

"This isn't happy news, but we're all gonna hold our heads high and manage our way through it." Hulda met eyes with each person around the table and issued her instructions. "I want each of you to pretend this was planned. Do your best to shut down any gossip the moment you hear it.

"I can't believe she did this to us, but we can get through it. We have no choice. Regina has brought shame to our family, and now it is ours to bear."

Regina got up the next morning and helped with breakfast as if nothing had changed. Herman and the boys wouldn't look at her, and they ate and left for the field as quickly as they could. To my knowledge, no one in the family discussed the matter after that night at supper. But whenever Regina appeared, the tension in the room was thick enough to taste.

Despite Hulda and the family's best efforts, gossip around town was rampant. Regina was not invited to any card parties, church circles, or any other social gathering. In fact, when she entered a room, folks scampered to get as far away from her as possible. Even though we tried to act as if nothing was different, no one could ignore Regina's expanding belly and the obviously promiscuous behavior that caused it.

One day, Hulda had gone to town with Herman to get some supplies, so Regina and I were alone in the house. With the winter wind blowing outside, and I had taken refuge in my quiet little corner by the stove. Regina came into the kitchen and sat near me. She stared into the fire.

"Shadow, I'm so alone. I wish I could go back in time and undo everything. But no matter how hard I pray, this baby keeps growing inside me, announcing my shame. I didn't understand what I was doing until it was too late.

"Remember that emptiness I told you about? It followed me to the city. But it was even worse when I got there. I had Ma's cousin to keep me company, but that was all.

"The city was big, and things moved so fast. I was afraid to leave the house alone. I thought I would get lost. Then one night we were invited to a ball. Can you imagine? A real ball with music and dancing, just like Johanna always talked about. We got dressed up in beautiful gowns and made up our faces.

"That night, I danced with so many good-looking young men. I batted my eyes and flipped my hair just like Johanna taught me. It worked so well. I felt that emptiness start to disappear as more and more boys asked me to dance. So I kept it up, that night and for the days and nights that followed.

"I had so many gentleman callers I started to lose track. I went walking with every one of them that asked, too. Ma's cousin warned me that people were starting to talk, but I didn't care. I just wanted these men to keep the emptiness away.

"Then one night, I let things go too far. At first I didn't know what he was doing. Then I didn't care. I felt swept away with passion.

"After that first time, there were many more to follow. I'm not proud of what I did, but I don't think I had control of myself, either. I just wanted more. It seemed to be the only thing that could make me feel whole again. When Ma's cousin got wind of what was going on, she bought me a train ticket and sent me home."

I sat by the fire listening to her. I felt my face grow red. I didn't want to hear these things. I didn't want to know these details, but she just kept talking. I sat quietly, listening as I always do. But inside I just wanted to run and hide.

"Shadow, now I'm more empty than I could ever have imagined possible," Regina sobbed. "No one will talk to me. Heck, they can hardly look at me. I hope this baby comes soon so things can get back to the way they were."

The little baby girl was born in March. Regina named her Adeline. She was a blonde-haired, blue-eyed little doll. She definitely took after Regina and was a happy baby just like her mama was as a child.

As much as Hulda would have liked to resist that baby, she was helpless. Soon that baby was doted on just as Regina had been at that age.

Sadly, things didn't get back to normal for Regina as she'd hoped. People in town still avoided her. The pastor refused to baptize Adeline, and the little one had to be taken to the church in the next township to get her divine blessing.

Regina quickly got her figure back, but there were still no callers. Mothers warned their girls to stay away from her for fear their own daughters would get ideas. It was a lonely time for Regina.

She seemed to have lost interest in everything. There were days when I would arrive in the morning to find Regina still in bed and she would sometimes go back to sleep again before supper. She rarely smiled anymore and if it wasn't for Hulda, I think little

Adeline would have died of neglect. If she spoke at all, it was only a whisper and she rarely went outdoors.

Late one summer evening when Adeline was about five months old, Regina and I were sitting out on the front porch. After supper, I grabbed her hand and was able to coax her out of her room. I was doing some mending while we watched the little one play with some rocks. A young couple stopped by asking directions to the Kasper Schmidt farm. Regina told them how to get there and seemed to enjoy a bit of conversation with the strangers as the night came on.

The woman said, "My! What a beautiful child! She is as sweet as they come. I hope one day to have a baby half as precious. You're a very lucky mother. Your husband must be so happy with his family."

"There is no husband, ma'am," said Regina. "This little girl is my bastard child."

The couple recoiled at such harsh and foul language. I did, too. I didn't know Regina thought such things much less would blurt them aloud to strangers.

"Oh, heavens," the woman gasped.

"That is no way to talk in front of a lady, miss," said the man angrily. "And you certainly have no cause to use such language in front of this precious little one. You should be ashamed of yourself."

"Oh, you don't need to lecture me about shame. This thing has given me more than a lifetime of shame. If you like her so much, why don't you just take her?"

"You must be joking!" exclaimed the woman.

I had never seen this side of Regina. She was not sad, hurt, or lost. She was angry and determined.

She said, "I'm serious. Adeline is her name, and she has brought me nothing but pain. You seem like nice people. Take her. PLEASE!"

The man and woman exchanged glances, and without a word between them, the woman picked up Adeline and the man helped them both into the wagon. They headed down the road.

I couldn't believe what I had just witnessed. I didn't believe what I was seeing. I wanted to stop it, but I didn't know how. Was it even my place? I felt as if I might vomit. I looked at Regina to see her reaction.

I expected her to be watching the wagon as it made its way down the road, but she wasn't. She just picked up the mending I was working on and took it over. Her face was drained of color, and she had a serious, almost determined look on her face. She saw me watching her and said very quietly, evenly, and without emotion, "Don't judge me."

I quickly looked down at the shirt in my lap that was in need of a patch. Was I judging her? I couldn't concentrate, I just sat beside her on the porch, watching the wind blow through the field.

Hulda came home from the neighbors a couple hours later, and Herman came in from the field a few minutes after that. They didn't notice Adeline's disappearance at first, but as Hulda put the kettle on the stove to heat up some water for coffee, she looked around for her little granddaughter.

"Where's Adeline?" she said to Regina.

Regina said firmly, "I gave her away."

"What? What do you mean?"

"I mean just what I said. I gave her to a nice young couple who stopped to get directions to the Kasper Schmidt place. They seemed to really like her, and I didn't want her anymore."

"What has gotten into you, child?" said Hulda.

Herman stood slack-jawed.

"Well, don't just stand there!" Hulda yelled. "Hitch up the wagon. We have to get to Kasper Schmidt's and hope Adeline is still there."

Herman seemed relieved to be given direction and left the house immediately to ready the horses.

Hulda turned to me. "Shadow, how *could* you have let this happen?"

I looked at the floor. I should have done something. Why didn't I do something? Even to this day I regret my inaction. That had always been my role, though. Just to watch and listen, never to participate or intervene. How I wished I was someone else. Someone better.

Back then, when a woman had a baby, she was meant to be filled with joy and get right back to work caring for her family. Nowadays, we know that sometimes new mothers get something called the baby blues. Looking back, I'm sure that was what Regina suffered from, especially because she had been so sad for so long before the birth.

Hulda glared at Regina and said, "We're going to bring Adeline home, and you will never give her away again. We will not speak of this, ever."

Hulda and Herman left and returned with little Adeline. True to Hulda's declaration, I did not hear the incident mentioned again. And that is a very odd thing given the way the town likes to talk. I think Hulda must have done some magic at Kasper Schmidt's that night to keep news like that from spreading.

Regina did eventually grow to be a good mother. As both Adeline and Regina matured, they developed an almost sisterly relationship. Regina the older, wiser, protective sister to the sweet, obedient, younger Adeline.

Hulda, of course, was the mother and authority of all. She made no secret of her devotion to them both and all settled into a routine soon enough.

Regina finally found her true love, and wouldn't you know, he had been a part of her life almost her whole life. Kasper Schmidt's second oldest son, Ignatz, said he took notice of her from the time he was ten years old and taught the little five-year-old Regina to make mud pies.

He waited patiently to start courting her until he felt he could offer her the life she deserved. He didn't seem bothered in the least that Regina had a baby out of wedlock or that taking her as his wife would instantly make him a father as well.

Ignatz and Regina decided to move out West shortly after they married. They loaded up little three-year-old Adeline and boarded the Northern Pacific Rail to Seattle.

Ignatz got a job almost immediately at a timber mill, and as soon as Adeline was old enough to go to school, Regina started working part time at a little store around the block from their place selling odds and ends to her neighbors and penny candy to the children. Eventually the couple bought the shop and worked there together.

About once a year they came home for a two-week visit. They talked on and on about how wonderful Seattle was. They tried to convince everyone what a full and successful life they were leading on the coast and begged everyone to come visit them.

After one such visit from Regina and Ignatz, I was pulling the last of the jars of beans out of the canner. Hulda and I put up over a dozen quarts that day, and she said I could take a couple back to my place after we finished up. I smiled and nodded. Then I waved for her to go outside and sit for a bit. She did so willingly.

As I cleaned up, I overheard Hulda and Herman talking quietly on the front porch as the sun went down. Hulda said, "Regina asked me to visit her. She said I could go on the train."

"Hmmm. I heard her go on about it."

"I told her it was too expensive and we didn't have money to go on a pleasure trip. But she said her and Ignatz talked about it, and they'd pay for my ticket."

"There's a lot of work to be done 'round here," Herman replied.

"I told her that, too, but she said Shadow could manage the place for a couple weeks."

"I 'spose she could. She's been workin' 'longside you since we homesteaded."

"I do miss those girls somethin' fierce," Hulda murmured in a rare moment of tenderness.

"Well, that settles it, then. Why don't you plan to go out after the harvest in late September? You can visit for a couple weeks and with luck be back before the snow flies."

"I haven't been on a train since we homesteaded, it's a long journey by myself. What if something happens?"

"Woman, you've never let anything stand in the way of gettin' what you want. You need to put that silly fear of trains behind you."

The next few weeks, Hulda was in rare form. She had me scrubbing every inch of the house, and we were putting up vegetables and making jam late into the evening. She kept complaining about how she had to do twice the work as usual so she wouldn't leave the place in shambles and the men to starve.

By the time she was ready for the trip, I was worn clean through.

Herman and the boys took her to the train and saw her off. I stayed back home to make sure supper would be on the table when they returned.

I remember how I enjoyed being in charge of the house. I didn't dare do anything differently than Hulda would have, but it felt good to manage my own schedule. I took pride in keeping things clean and serving the meals on schedule.

I think I would have made a good wife and mother if things had been different. I loved my little house and was happy there. But being on the farm taking care of Herman and the boys by myself made me long for the way things might have been instead of the way they were. I guess that's how life works out sometimes. There's no use dwelling on it.

When Hulda got back from her trip, I had a nice hot meal of her favorites already set on the table as the wagon pulled up. Fried chicken, white gravy, mashed potatoes, peas, and apple pie for dessert. She didn't even bother to take her things out of her trunk before she sat down and started eating.

"It's 'bout time I had some real food in my system," she said between mouthfuls. "Regina was feedin' me all sorts of things I never heard of before, much less put in my mouth. She kept sneaking this stuff she called crab into everythin'. Crab in my eggs, crab in my sandwich, and even crab in the stew! She acted like it was really somethin'."

"What is crab?" said Jack.

"Darned if I could figure it out. Near as I could tell it's the meat from some sort of animal, but it sure isn't any animal we ever raised on the farm. It has a sort of sweet taste and a real funny smell. I didn't think I would ever get that scent outta my nose!"

"Was it good?" Herman asked.

"Well, I don't know. How could I say if it was good or not? I don't even know what it is, and she kept telling me to go sit and relax in the other room when she was cookin'. She said it was time she waited on me for a change. That I was her guest. But there's only so much relaxin' a body can take. I was wore out from relaxin'!"

Over the next few weeks, Hulda told of her trip to Seattle in much the same complaining way to everyone who would listen.

After church that first Sunday, Lydia said, "But how was the scenery, Hulda? I hear that train ride is beautiful."

"Well, I heard that, too, and I kept lookin'. But I couldn't see any scenery. There were just too many mountains and trees blockin' the view!"

That was the only time Hulda made the trip west. She must have gotten over her fear of train travel though because she sent Jack out to visit Regina a few times. She said that a mind as active as his should experience as much of the world as it could.

Regina had three more children with Ignatz. She named all three boys after birds, Robin, Finch and Lark. It likely won't surprise you that Hulda did not approve of these names. She said on many occasions, "Those poor boys. Those names are the influence of that uppity Johanna Malsom, God rest her soul. I shouldn't have allowed Regina to spend so much time with her." I rather liked the names but I did think they would have been better suited to girls.

I only met the boys a couple of times. A few years after her youngest was born, Regina and Ignatz cut their visits to every other year and then every third. They left the boys back in Washington with a neighbor friend. She said the boys didn't like the long train ride but I suspected Ignatz couldn't afford their train tickets.

Regina and her family lived in Seattle until she died. I believe she had a happy life. At least that's the way it sounded in the Christmas letters she sent to me every year. She was buried next to her husband. I was told that Adeline planted a lilac bush next to their graves.

Adeline married quite young, and we heard she had a baby soon after the wedding. Maybe too soon, some said when Hulda was out of earshot. She moved to Portland, and we didn't hear much from her after that.

The Storm

I haven't written anything for a while. Of course, there are other stories that I could share with you, but the truth is, I'm tired. Writing my memories down like this has taken a toll on me. I find that as I get older, my hands ache and cramp from the arthritis that has taken over the joints of my fingers. It flares up if I hold the pencil too long. I've also become more emotional, and some of these memories have haunted me longer than they should have. I think it's time for me to finish.

But there's one more story I'm going to write. I thought all the stories were in the past, but maybe not. God gave me one more, but unlike the others, this one is likely special only to me. There may be dark days ahead when I'll pull this story out and read it. Or there may be no days ahead. At this point in life, we just don't know. But this last story will always be close to my heart. So I'll write it, and then I'll have finished what God asked me to start so many months ago.

It was Saturday afternoon. I was listening to the news on my little television. The weather man broke in to my program and started talking about a major winter storm that was coming our way. I looked out the window and could definitely see the sky in the west getting darker. The wind was picking up. Two inches of fluffy snow fell last Wednesday, and the wind was already blowing that around, creating a bit of a ground blizzard. As so often happens during these first weeks of January, the temperature has dropped to a dangerous level. My thermometer reads 20 below air temperature, and with the wind chill, it likely feels closer to 50 below.

I couldn't help but think how different it is to live in these modern times than in the years of my youth. The times and most of the people in the stories I wrote about are all long gone. Nowadays, women are wearing pants, almost everyone has a car, and people eat as many meals at the café as they do at home. Yes, the 1960s are vastly different from the 1880s.

Back then, we used to get up early and start cooking. Everything was made on a wood stove. Now a wife can get up at the same time as her husband. The coffee is made in a percolator, and a meal can be thrown together in no time with a can of soup, a pound of hamburger, and some rice. No need to collect the wood and start a fire; just turn the dial and the heat is on. That gives you about an hour to get your other chores done while it cooks. After the supper dishes are done, a woman can sit with her family and listen to the radio or watch the television. Electricity is used for everything and has made life so much easier.

A few years back, Jack had a bathroom built on the east side of my little house, just off the living room. At first he wanted to put it off the kitchen, but I refused. I thought it was unnecessary to have a toilet indoors, much less next to where you cook and eat your meals. However, on a cold, dark winter day like we had last Saturday, I sure was glad not to have to brave the elements.

Over the years, my little home became a sort of pet project for the church. The congregation helped to replace the original sod foundation with cement brick and wood. New windows, electricity, and plumbing were installed along the way, too. The floorplan is still pretty much the same, but the structure is completely different.

As I sat by the wood stove in the living room, reflecting on all the changes I'd witnessed in my life, I heard a familiar knock on my door. It was David. Since his Doris died, I've been seeing more of him. I feel sorry for him because he misses her so deeply, but I can't say I don't enjoy his more frequent visits.

After he finished high school, he started the International Harvester Dealership with the help of his father. Over the years he proved he had a real head for business, and his reputation for being fair and honest with the farmers spread through this part of the state.

He's retired now, of course, but at seventy-two he still goes in to the shop for a few hours most days to visit with the customers. One of his salesmen bought him out, and it seems as if their friendship strengthened after the sale.

I smiled at David and motioned for him to come in. I wanted to get the door closed as quickly as I could. The wind was strong and bitterly cold as it blew the snowflakes into the entrance.

He took off his red dealership jacket and the crocheted stocking hat that Doris made for him several years ago.

I pointed to a chair by the table for him to sit and then plugged the pot in for coffee. Usually when David stopped by, he would stay for an hour or so and tell me the news from town. So as the coffee was percolating, I turned the television down and took a seat at the table.

David saw the pile of paper on the little buffet I keep in the corner of the kitchen and grabbed a sheet. He held it up to me and asked in his gravelly voice, "Shadow, have you been writing something? Would you mind if I read it?"

I shrugged and nodded, letting him know that I didn't care. If he wanted to look over the stories, there would be no harm. I thought that no one on those pages would mind if I shared their stories now. And since the good Lord asked me to put these things down, He must have intended for someone to read them.

As David began to flip through the pages, he started to smile. "This is about all of us. Huh! I've half forgotten some of these people. What the heck made you think to write all this down anyway?"

Again, I just shrugged. As David read, I got up from the table and busied myself making a batch of cookies. I thought David might enjoy something to go along with his coffee, and the way he was settling in his chair, I could tell he was in no hurry to leave.

It wasn't long and there was another knock at the door. This time it was Jack. Except for the mess the wind made out of his combed over hair, he looked quite handsome standing there in his stylish green plaid pants and matching turtleneck sweater. Hulda would've had a fit over those pants. I can hear her now. "Jack, a man of your stature shouldn't be walkin' around with flashy pants like that!" I often hear her in my head when I see Jack. The two of them butted heads so often, but in the most loving way possible.

Jack greeted me in the deep voice that made him such a good speaker. "Hello, Shadow. I was driving by and wanted to see if you needed anything. They say this storm is going to be a bad one, and with as cold as it is, you shouldn't be out fetchin' anything."

I motioned for him to come in.

When he saw David, a broad smile came over his clean-shaven face. "David! I thought that might be your rig out there. Good to see you!"

The two men shook hands as Jack came in and sat down at the table across from David. I grabbed two cups and poured the freshly brewed coffee into them. I ran to the icebox and pulled out

Hulda's porcelain cow-shaped creamer that poured milk from the cow's mouth.

After Hulda passed, her children asked if there was anything I wanted. That cow creamer was the only thing I took. I set it down alongside the sugar bowl. Jack liked his coffee with milk and sugar, while David always drank his black. David often joked, "I like my coffee like I like my women, strong and black!" That always made Doris, who was very blonde and pale, laugh out loud, no matter how many times she heard him say it.

"Say, Jack, did you know Shadow here has been telling stories on us?" David said as he winked at me.

Jack looked at me. "What's that, now?"

I grinned and pointed at the pile of paper that David had in front of him. David slid the pile across the table for Jack to see.

"Well, I'll be!" As Jack started to read, he began to chuckle. "Boy, I sure did give Ma a hard time!"

"You don't need to worry about Hulda," David shot back, "That woman gave as good as she got!"

All three of us smiled at that. Hulda had a way with people. She was as ornery as they come and never held back her opinion on anything, but she also had the biggest, most generous heart you ever saw.

Herman died of a heart attack about thirty-five years ago now. Hulda moved to town, and Val, their eldest boy, took over the farm. After Herman passed, Hulda continued to sit in the third pew on the left side every Sunday at church. I sat next to her. Noreen sat on her other side, and eventually Lydia joined us. That pew became known as Gray Hair Row.

Hulda was full of spit until the day she died. Those other women are all gone now, too, leaving me to occupy the pew alone. Well, not alone actually. Jack's big family takes up the better part of all the first three rows.

After high school, Jack was drafted and left the farm to join the Army. He graduated as valedictorian of the class and hoped to go to college. It was a big dream. No one from that one room schoolhouse had ever gone off to a university before. But, the draft gave him no choice but to serve his country like all the other young men of the time. Thankfully, he served in between the wars and didn't see any action, as they say. What he did find, though, was religion.

Even though Hulda always made sure that her children were dressed properly and sitting straight and respectfully in church on Sunday, Jack told me that he didn't really *feel* God's presence in his life until one day when he was very homesick at boot camp. He was sometimes picked on by the others, who called him a " smart aleck country boy." He confided that he sometimes felt so alone and hopeless that he wasn't sure he could go on. He snuck away from the mess hall one day when he was feeling particularly down and went to the chapel to think. He wanted to talk to someone but no one was there. He got down on his knees and prayed for the Lord to lift his burden and show him the way.

"Shadow, I know it's gonna sound crazy, but I actually FELT Him. There was a sort of chill that ran through me. Sort of like that feeling just after you sneeze, but stronger. It only lasted a few seconds, but after that, I was changed. The chaplain came in, and I talked with him about what had just happened. Over the next few months, he helped me see that I was being called."

After his time in the service, Jack went to seminary and became a pastor. Hulda couldn't contain her pride when she bragged about Jack's higher education and his calling. Jack met a girl at the same college who was studying to be a nurse. They fell in love and got married just about the same time the pastor at our little church here retired. The congregation put out a call, and with Hulda's urging, Jack was installed without resistance.

I love sitting in the pew on Sunday mornings with his family. His four boys and their wives, his grandchildren, and in just the past few years even a few great-grandchildren sit with me to listen to Jack preach. He's good, too. Although sometimes it's hard not to remember the stubborn little boy he used to be.

Two Sundays ago he was delivering a sermon on the commandment, "Thou shalt honor thy mother and thy father." I had to cover my face with a hanky so no one would see me chuckling.

As David and Jack settled in at the table, I put the first batch of cookies in the oven. Most people nowadays put chocolate chips in cookies. I find them to be too sweet. I prefer the oatmeal Rice Krispies cookies that Lydia always made. She isn't around to make them anymore, and I miss her a little less when I smell a batch baking.

Every time I taste a little of the raw cookie dough, I'm transported straight back to her kitchen in the late twenties. Theophil bought her one of the first ovens in the state, and she collected as many new recipes as she could get her hands on. These cookies were among her favorites, and she made them often.

I think Hulda might have been a little jealous of that oven. I would often hear her mumbling as she stoked her own fire with wood and coal, "All these newfangled machines just get in the way. I wouldn't even want one clutterin' up my kitchen."

It was only a few years later that Herman surprised her by bringing one home strapped in the back of his Model T Ford Runabout truck. Hulda ran from the house and nearly toppled him over in an unexpected, aggressive, and uncharacteristic embrace. Herman and the boys were so surprised at her reaction they almost fell over laughing as they carried it in the house and got it hooked up.

I had just handed the two men a plate with a couple of the warm cookies that I just pulled from the oven when there was another knock at the door. You may find it surprising that I have so much company. Since the highway was built on the edge of my land, people are always driving by. You can see my place from the road, and with the town growing like it is, I'm now only about a mile from town.

I left the pan of cookies I was preparing to go in next and opened the door. It was Elmer, Theophil's oldest grandson. He wasn't so much a boy now as a grown man of forty with a wife and child of his own. He took over the farm when his folks retired and moved to town about ten years back.

Just like his grandpa, he was a hard worker and loved to tell a good story. He was doing real good on the farm, too. Elmer was smart and had a sense about what to plant, when to harvest, and when to sell to get the best price.

Standing there at my door with his striped bib overalls and short-sleeved denim shirt covering his white long johns, he was the spitting image of his grandfather. He even inherited Theophil's slow prairie accent.

As he entered the house, he removed the DeKalb feed store cap he always wore when he went out. "Evenin', Shadow. We was just done butcherin' a cow, and I figured I'd run over with a coupla roasts for ya before the snow started."

He joined me at the window and looked outside. "I wasn't fast enough, though, cause it's already coming down. Looks like we're in for a good one, not?" He nodded at the table. "How ya doin', Reverend, David. Whatta ya up to with all that paperwork?"

"Come on and sit down a spell, son," Jack invited. "David and I had the same idea as you, I guess. We all stopped by to make sure Shadow was set to survive the storm, and before we knew it, she had us sitting here at her table drinking coffee and eating cookies."

"Mmmmm. I guess I'd know that smell anywhere. Those are my grandma's cookies, not? I keep telling the wife to get that recipe from you, Shadow, but she says, 'A cookie isn't a cookie without a chip.' She has all those modern ideas about things like that," he said with exaggerated remorse.

David handed him a few pages. "You're gonna wanna read some of this. It's your family history, is what it is."

As I poured a cup of coffee for Elmer and refilled the other cups, I looked outside again. The snow had really started coming down, and the wind was whipping it so hard I had trouble seeing the highway sign at the end of my drive. I put my hand on David's shoulder to get his attention and pointed outside.

"It's a bad one, all right." He looked from one man to the other. "I think we best wait it out, don't you?"

"This is as good a place as any to be stuck in a blizzard, I guess," said Jack, seeming to sense David's need for company. "Whatta you say, Elmer? Should we just hunker down 'til it blows over?"

Elmer nodded right away. "I was thinkin' the same thing. It was drizzlin' before the snow started, and the road comin' in is pure ice. Even in my truck, I was slidin' all over the place. I wasn't lookin' forward to the drive back. I'll just call the wife and let her know where I am."

Jack stood. "I'll do the same."

David sighed. "No one's waiting on me back home. I guess that's the benefit of being a bachelor again: no one checkin' up on you."

"We all miss her, David. Your Doris was one in a million, that's for sure," Jack said quietly as he placed a hand on his friend's shoulder to comfort him.

I bet you're wondering why a woman who doesn't talk has a telephone. I can't believe it myself, but I didn't have much choice. About ten years ago, Jack came over with one of the men from the phone company to install it. He didn't ask. He just showed up and had it put in. I tried to stop him, but he said, "Now Shadow, you're out here all by yourself, and you need to have a way to reach someone if you need help."

I shook my head and pointed to my throat. I wondered if he forgot that I don't talk.

"I know, Shadow. We developed a system. If you need help, you call one of our numbers. I wrote them all on this paper. You dial and let it ring once and hang up. Then you call back and let it ring twice and hang up. That'll be the signal. I already worked it out with David and Doris and all of our clan—and Theophil's, too. If you get into any kinda trouble, you just signal one of us on this list, and we'll be by in a jiffy."

I gave up. The thing just sits there collecting dust until someone comes by and wants to make a call. On a day like today, though, I have to admit, it sure is nice to have. It'll go a long way to take the worry off the shoulders of Jack's and Elmer's wives.

As the two men made their calls, David asked me where he should begin reading. I went to the table and put the mess of papers back in order as best I could and pointed to the top page.

Soon, David was reading aloud in his gravelly voice as the other two sat looking at him like the little boys I remembered them both being. It warmed my heart to have these men in my kitchen. David had been my friend as long as I could remember. Jack was like a little brother to me, and Elmer was the spitting image of his grandfather, Theophil—who'd been my best friend when I was just a wee thing myself.

As David was reading the story of Theophil's journey across the prairie, he suddenly stopped. "I remember that dang old cow, Lily!" He laughed and looked at Elmer. "Your grandpa pampered that animal like she was one of his own kids. I was there the day he had to put her down. I went over to see if I could convince one of their boys to go fishin' with me. I saw that big man standin' there lookin' at that animal with tears rolling down his cheeks, snifflin' like a baby. We cleared outta the yard for fear he'd be so blurry eyed that he might mistake one of us for that cow and shoot the wrong one. I was too young then to understand what that cow must've meant to him."

Elmer chuckled. "You know, I remember Grandpa Theophil talking 'bout a Lily. I couldn't figure out why the heck he kept talkin' 'bout an old girlfriend that way and why Grandma didn't get mad. I never woulda guessed that Lily was a cow!"

We were all laughing then, remembering what a tender heart Theophil had.

As David continued reading and the men continued to discuss the stories I'd written, adding their own memories every so often, I set about making the roasts that Elmer had brought.

I peeled some potatoes and carrots, chopped an onion, and put the vegetables and meat in my roasting pan with plenty of salt and pepper. A little water in the bottom and into the oven it went. As supper was cooking, I poured myself a cup of coffee and joined the men at the table. I had at least a couple hours before I would need to start on dessert.

As David read about Lydia's sister, Emma, and how she broke Theophil's heart, I felt a lump in my throat. It was a long time ago, but I still remembered it clearly. Elmer and Jack listened intently. They didn't interrupt the reading, but the way they looked at each other and then at me, I could tell this was a story they weren't familiar with.

David had to stop a few times in his reading as his voice caught in his throat. I poured him a glass of water, and after a quick drink, he said he remembered running into Theophil that day at the picnic when he was a young boy. It was one of his very earliest memories. He said that beet juice really made a mess out of Theophil's clothes. "I thought I was gonna get yelled at, but all of a sudden everyone was laughin'. I couldn't figure out what happened, but I remember sitting extra quiet on the way home that day. Ma and Pa were always tellin' me to quit actin' so squirrely."

Jack added, "I remember hearing the boys talk about an Aunt Emma when I was over there. I don't think they ever met her, but they heard so many stories about her from their Ma, I think they felt like they did. She and Theophil talked about her with such tenderness, even though I always felt there was something more about her that they weren't saying."

He turned to Elmer and said, "Your grandparents had a way of talking to each other with just their eyes. I envied that. They had a sort of secret language. And the way they treated each other was really something. I always hoped that some day I would find a girl that would look at me the way Lydia looked at Theophil. He didn't make any secret of how he felt about her, either. That kind of love is rare. They were sure lucky that Aunt Emma changed her mind!"

Elmer said, "I didn't know that story, either, but I sure am thankful that Grandpa got over that heartbreak. I wouldn't be here today if he hadn't." He looked at me and said, "Thank you, Shadow, for being such a good friend to him. For not givin' up on him. It couldn't have been easy sittin' with him all that time."

I felt my face grow hot. I was uncomfortable with his gratitude. I didn't do anything. I don't even speak. I was just there. That's all. I didn't deserve thanks. I got up from the table and started busying myself in the kitchen again. It was about time for me to get dessert started, and I didn't want anymore attention. Plus, I knew the story they were about to read next. I wondered if I would be able to bear hearing his name read aloud after all these years. Nicklaus. My Nicklaus. Yet, I had a strange feeling that I wanted these men to know this story.

David began to read aloud again. When he reached the part of the story that described the day I met my Nicklaus, Jack interrupted. "Hey, wait just a minute, David. I remember you telling me to run around the church yard so you could time me. You stole that trick from this Nicklaus guy, didn't you?!"

David laughed. "I remember that day in town when Nicklaus had me running my fool head off. I had no idea that he wanted to flirt with you, Shadow. I remember I was feeling kinda protective of you. Like you were my special friend, and I didn't like sharin' you with 'im. But Nicklaus had such a way 'bout him that I liked him right away, so I decided I didn't mind him being around after all. "

He turned to Jack. "If you recall, I was doin' a bit of flirtin' myself that day I told you I would time you. You kept comin' over and askin' me to go play catch with you. I had other things on my mind and had to get rid of you somehow. That trick worked just as good for me as it did for Nicklaus, I guess. I had you runnin' 'round that church so many times, your ma had to help you to the wagon. As she carried you off, she shot me a look that coulda killed a horse. Hulda knew what I had on my mind."

The three men laughed heartily at the memory. They all exchanged a few more stories about the girls they were sweet on and the foolish things they did to try to get their attention.

Soon enough though, David started to read about the day of the drownings. He, too, knew what was coming and paused for a moment. He looked at me and with misty eyes said, "Funny how something like that can stick with you your whole life. Sometimes, on a beautiful spring day, I close my eyes, and it's as if I'm back there again. That first warm day of the year should be something to celebrate, but on days like that, I always seem to feel melancholy."

I couldn't look at him. I swallowed hard, put my hand on his, and nodded slightly so he'd know I felt the same.

He excused himself to go to the bathroom, and I started to clear the papers away and set the table for supper. I thought it best to eat first. The storm wasn't letting up. In fact, it sounded as if the wind was blowing even harder. There would be plenty of time to finish that story after we ate.

With the supper on the table and after a blessing from Jack, we all started dishing up the food. As I watched the men fill their plates, I had a moment of panic. I wondered if I'd made enough food. I'm so used to cooking only for myself that I sometimes forget how big a man's appetite can be. I quickly realized that worrying about it wouldn't do any good. I didn't have much more in the house, and with the storm continuing to build outside, we'd just have to make do with what was on the table.

David looked at Elmer. "What's that little guy of yours been up to lately? He must be five by now."

Elmer grinned as he always did when talking about his only son. "Well, Hank's actually six now, seven in a coupla months. He's in the dog house with the wife at the moment. It might be colder in that house than it is outside tonight! I don't mind sayin' I was happy to get outta there for a while."

"Why's that?" Jack asked.

Elmer chuckled. "We had Elaine and Vern Bieber over to the house last night to play cards. Hank came to the table and joined us when we was takin' a break to have a little coffee cake. That boy always seems to show up when somethin' sweet is brought out.

"Well, Elaine looks over at him and says, 'What's that look on your face, Hank? Whattaya thinkin' about?'

"He says back to her, 'I'm just wishin' I was growed up so I could finally do what I wanna do!'

"So, Elaine asks him, 'Well, what do you want to do, Hank?'

"Without skipping a beat, my boy looks up all serious and announces loud and clear, 'I wanna CUSS!'

"The wife got all embarrassed and started scoldin' him. 'Hank, that's no way to talk!' she says.

"Hank looks over to Elaine like he's pleadin' for her to help. 'See what I mean! The teacher says we live in a free country, and that means we can say whatever we want and not get in trouble. But around here, we don't have freedom. She's always tellin' us what we can't do!'

"Now the wife is gettin' hot. 'That's enough, Hank!' she says.

"'I'm right, though. Dad, I'm right, aren't I?'"

Elmer was laughing now. "The wife was lookin' at me like she was fit to string both of us up. So, I says, 'Hank, I think it's time for bed, not?'

"I took him to bed and got him tucked in, but when I went back out to finish the game, the wife looked like she just sucked on a lemon. I don't have to tell you that the Biebers called it a night earlier than usual."

As Elmer told us about the previous night, I couldn't help but think of his grandfather, Theophil. The two men were so much alike. They looked alike, had the same manner of speech, and both loved to entertain a group with a humorous story.

After the laughter around my table died down a bit, Jack said, "Does Hank like school? He's going full days this year, right?"

Elmer smiled, "Well, that's another thing."

We couldn't help but to snicker a bit in anticipation for whatever Elmer was about to tell us next.

"Back in September, I come in to see how his first day went. There was little Hank, sittin' at the table drinkin' some cocoa and eatin' some cinnamon and sugar toast. He still had his coat on.

" 'Well, how'd it go?' I says.

" 'Oh, Dad, it wasn't good.'

"'Whatdya mean?'

" 'Well, this mornin' I was walkin' down the driveway to the bus stop, mindin' my own business, when suddenly I stepped in poop! A really big pile, too, and it was fresh. I tried to get it all off by draggin' my foot in the grass, only it didn't help so much. It smelled all day. I was almost pukin'! When I got to my desk, the teacher walked by me and looked at my shoes. Then, she went to her desk and grabbed a paper bag and made me put it over my shoe. Everyone was laughin' at me.'

Elmer continued, "About a month after that he says to me, Ma is gonna have to give me a ride from now on.'

"'Why's that?' I says. 'You were wantin' to ride that yellow bus, not?'

"'Ya, but not now. Maybe in the summer, but its too dang cold to be ridin' that bus now.'

"'Hank, you better not let your ma hear you use words like that! And it's not even cold, it was only 40 this mornin'. It's gonna get a lot colder'n that. You gonna have to toughen up,' I told 'im.

"'But, Dad,' he whined, 'I was so cold, I couldn't feel my eyes…really!'

"He says it's so cold he can't feel his eyes! I don't know where he comes up with that stuff!" Elmer said shaking his head and laughing along with the rest of us.

I can't tell you the joy that filled me as I watched these three men laugh, eat, and tell stories at my table. I felt so blessed to have their warm and easy companionship in my kitchen as the storm raged outside.

After we finished eating, cleared the dishes, and wiped the table, David grabbed the stack of papers off the buffet and slid the pages across the table to Jack.

"Jack, I think I know what Shadow wrote about next. If I'm right, I'm not sure I can get through this next part. I think you best pick up the readin' from here."

As Jack grabbed the papers and adjusted his glasses, he glanced at Elmer and the two of them shared a confused look.

Before Jack could start reading, I turned my back to the men and busied myself at the sink. I was happy to be washing the dishes so they couldn't see my face.

Jack read about that day by the lake. The day so many lost their lives. Jack's clear, deep voice reading my love story aloud was both beautiful and heartwrenching. I made slow work of the dishes and didn't turn to face the table until the story was finished.

After Jack stopped reading, the men were quiet for quite some time, each apparently thinking his own thoughts about the impact that picnic had on this community.

I made another pot of coffee and poured each of us a cup. I sat back down in my chair at the table between Jack and Elmer. After a time, Jack broke the silence. "Shadow, you spoke?"

I gave him a slight smile and a small nod as I looked at my hands. Somehow I felt the same way I did when David said he had heard me speak that day at the lake, exposed, almost as if I were naked.

Again, there was a long pause in the conversation.

Jack spoke again. "I've heard people reference those drownings all my life. I know just where those trees are that Ma planted. I guess I knew about that day, but until right now, I'm ashamed to admit, I never really understood just how hard it must have been. I never thought of it as anything more than a sad story. Shadow, David, I'm so sorry for your losses. I'm so sorry for what you saw, and I'm so sorry you have to live with that memory. Would you mind if I said a prayer?"

No one said anything, but we all bowed our heads and held hands.

Jack began in his preaching voice, "Dear Lord, it is times like this when we realize just how short our lives are. We realize that we don't always understand Your plan for our lives. We know that we are not meant to understand. Lord, we also realize that we don't always see the pain and suffering that people bear on the inside. We only see the brave faces they show us on the outside.

Lord, open our hearts to provide love, comfort, and understanding to all those we meet. Let us live in the example of Your Son, Jesus Christ, who showed all he met caring and mercy. Lord, please hear our prayers and keep all those who died that day and all those who survived that day in Your good graces. Lord, thank You for bringing the brave and selfless Nicklaus into this community. Please hold him in Your grace as he waits for his Shadow, uh, Ray, to join him in their heavenly home. Amen."

Jack gave my hand a little squeeze before he let go. I got up and grabbed a box of tissues from the other room and set them on the table. Each of us grabbed one and chuckled a little as we blew our noses and wiped our eyes.

Once again we sat in silence for a bit, but this time it was Elmer who broke the silence.

"Did they ever find the teeth?" he said in a sad and serious tone.

"Teeth? What teeth?" David asked.

"The false teeth that the woman dropped?"

It was a full half minute before we all started laughing at him. Elmer looked from one of us to the other with a questioning look on his face and then suddenly started laughing as well.

As our laughter subsided, I realized I hadn't served dessert yet. I turned from the table and plugged in the percolator to make yet another pot of coffee. As I fussed around at the counter, Jack began to read aloud again. This time, he was reading about my Nicklaus's brother Kermit and his friend Pius.

As he began to read, David interrupted, shaking his head, "Kermit and Pius. Now those are names I haven't heard in a long while. Settle in boys, this is going to be quite a tale."

"Kermit and Pius?" Elmer questioned. "I don't think I ever heard those names before. They have any kin 'round here?"

"You know, I don't think I know those names either. Who are they, David?" Jack asked.

David explained that Kermit was my Nicklaus's brother. He told them that he and his friend, Pius, arrived some time after the drownings. Then he winked at me and said, "You keep readin' Jack. I'm sure Shadow wrote it all down."

I gave David a quizzical look. The story of Kermit and Pius wasn't a happy one. I couldn't figure out why he had a smirk on his face as if it was a fond memory.

Before Jack could begin reading again, David looked at me and said, "Shadow, I can see by the look on your face you're wonderin' what I'm thinkin' about. Well, I got a story 'bout these two that I bet even you don't know."

"Well, you best tell all of us, then," Jack replied.

"Okay," David started, "but I have to warn ya. You may discover just what kind of delinquent I was back then."

"You? A delinquent? Never! You were an example of goodness and kindness that we all had to live up to. I used to get so frustrated with your purity," Jack teased.

"Every time there was bad news to tell, you were always the one to come around and share it. After you left, Ma would start lecturing me and the whole family. 'That David Deis is a young man to model yerself after. He doesn't just lay around waitin' to be told what to do; he gets up and tries to help folks in times of difficulty. You all would do well to be more like him.' You set the standard so high that none of us stood a chance!"

David let out a deep belly laugh as Jack mimicked Hulda's voice. "I wasn't bein' good! I was just takin' advantage of a good situation!"

"I don't believe that for a second," Jack responded. "I was there when you told us that someone had been in an accident or died. You didn't look like you were enjoying yourself."

"Well, here's the truth of it," David confessed. "The first time I was asked to share some bad news I was about ten or so. It was harvest time and my dad and brothers had to get the field work done and my ma was busy puttin' up the vegetables from the garden, so she told me I had to go tell the neighbors. I complained and tried to get outta it, but Ma wouldn't budge. There was no one else to do it she said. So, off I went, sulkin' the whole way.

"Well, wouldn't you know, at every house I stopped at I was given somethin' to eat. You can see by the look of me now that I like to eat, but back when I was a boy, I ate even more." David patted his belly with a smile.

"From then on, I volunteered to go tell the bad news every chance I got. I learned that the more hang-dog I looked, the more I got fed! I even planned my route. I always started at your place, Jack. Hulda was the best cook around, and if I timed it right, she'd invite me to stay for supper. Then, I'd head over to your granma's place, Elmer. Lydia made the best kuchen I ever tasted. She'd put double custard in each crust and used a light touch when addin' the prunes.

"I swear, the year of the plague, I bet I gained 20 pounds!"

Jack chuckled. "I wish I would've known that back then. I could've stuck up for myself a little when Ma was hoisting you up on that pedestal."

"I wanna hear about this mischief you got into with these two fellas, Kermit and Pius," Elmer interjected as the chuckling started to subside.

"Okay, okay, I'll tell ya." David settled back into his chair.

"I was about thirteen years old when Kermit and Pius arrived. I was lookin' forward to bein' old enough to havin' some fun and feelin' some independence. When Kermit and Pius moved to town, they caused quite a stir. Everyone was talkin' about the newcomers, and all the girls in school were makin' goo-goo eyes at Pius. Us boys idolized them two. They were older, and we thought they were all it.

"My folks had the two of them to the house for supper a few times. I thought Kermit was a bit off, but I really liked Pius and would always try to impress him. I remember bringin' out all my wood carvings and such to show him. I tried anything to get his attention, hopin' he'd like me.

"Anyway, the church had some youth activity or somethin' that just got over one Saturday night and I was on my way home. I was walkin' down the road when I heard some footsteps comin' up fast behind me. I turned 'round, and here it was Kermit and Pius.

"Kermit says, 'Hey, kid, we need some help. You in?'

"I was both excited he was talkin' to me and nervous at what he wanted with me. But Pius piped up right away and told me not to worry. He'd be there, too, and would make sure nothin' went wrong.

"So I followed 'em over to ol' Kasper Schmidt's place. It was just about dusk by this time, and the shadows were gettin' longer. I asked 'em what they wanted me to do.

"Kermit starts in. 'I 'bout had enough of him talkin' 'bout things he has no business talkin' 'bout. He needs to learn to keep his mouth shut about me and my family. I'm gonna teach him a lesson, and you're gonna help me,' he says, all angry-like.

"Pius starts grinnin' and tells me that Kermit overheard ol' Kasper Schmidt tellin' someone in town that Kermit had a temper on 'im and sure wasn't the kinda upstandin' young man his brother was. He said somethin' 'bout a fire at a church back home or somethin'. I guess he went on a little 'fore he noticed Kermit was behind him, hearin' the whole thing. Pius tilted his head in Kermit's direction. 'He was madder than a cat in a rainstorm that night,' he says.

"Well, we get to the Schmidt place, and they lead me to the chicken coop. They tell me I have to crawl under the back of the coop wall, get inside, and steal that goose he's so proud of.

"I protested a little. I didn't wanna do it, but I also didn't wanna let these two older fellas down. I was proud they wanted my help even if it was just 'cause I was small enough to squeeze under the shed wall."

"Why didn't they just open the door of the coop and walk in?" Elmer wondered aloud.

"They couldn't go in from the front. Too risky. The coop was situated on the property so you could see the door of it from the picture window of the house. The Schmidt family was sittin' in the livin' room. We could see 'em in there starin' at the radio right in front of the window. So we knew they would see us.

"So while Kermit and Pius hid in the shelter belt off a ways, I creeped up behind the coop. I got down on my belly and squirmed my way under the the wall. I saw the goose right away, but it was a fat thing. I looked 'round and made out a shovel leanin' in the corner. I decided to dig the openin' I crawled through a little bigger so I could fit back through it as I crawled with that goose in my arms.

"I tell you, that goose was none too happy for me to grab it in the dark and try to wrassle it under that wall. It was honkin' and flappin' its wings and makin' a racket. It somehow found the tender skin under my arm with its beak and grabbed on tight. It pinched and twisted so hard I couldn't help but to let out a squeal.

"I finally got out with the bird only to drop it in the yard. It took off runnin' 'round the yard as I ran after it and finally fell on top of it. By the time I had control of it and found Kermit and Pius, they were rollin' around on the grass laughin' their fool heads off.

"By now I was covered in dirt and chicken poop, and I could feel a bruise the sized of a watermelon startin' to develop under my arm. I was mad. I threw the bird at Kermit and started walking toward home. I didn't know how I was gonna explain my appearance to my folks. In the end, I just didn't say a word to 'em. I just shook my head and told my ma I didn't wanna talk about it. You can bet I got punished for that!"

"Well, that's some story, David!" Jack said.

David raised his eyebrows. "Oh, I'm not through yet."

"Next day after church, ol' Kasper Schmidt comes up to me in the yard and tells my ma he needs to talk privately to me. Ma was confused, but she told me to go on. I could feel my face gettin' red with the shame I was feelin' for stealin' his goose.

"He gets me aside, and he says, 'David, I know you stole that goose last night. You don't need to bother tryin' to deny it. I know it was you. I also know you aren't a bad kid, and someone musta put you up to it. Now, you know there are a lot a folks around here that don't have much. Shoot, I'm one of 'em. But I got more'n most, and I been raisin' that goose for the annual Thanksgivin' supper at the church. I promised to provide the meat for that meal, and without that goose, more'n a few are gonna go without. Now, I know you don't want to be responsible for that. So here's what's gonna happen. You're gonna return that goose to the chicken coop by the time the sun goes down tonight. So long as that goose is there tomorrow morning when I go out to feed the chickens, I won't say a word to no one. Understand, me?'

"Oh, I understood him. But what could I do? I didn't know where Kermit and Pius took that goose, and my ma was watchin' me like a hawk. As ol' Kasper was tellin' me he saw me steal his goose, my ma was telling the ladies she didn't know how she was gonna get my clothes clean after my escapade the night before. It wasn't likely I was gonna be free anytime soon."

"Whadja do?" Elmer prompted.

"As luck would have it, I overheard your granpa Theophil tellin' my pa that Kermit gave him a big fat goose that mornin'. Kermit tol' him it was a thank-you for borrowin' him some tools he needed to finish the house. That's how I knew where to find that goose.

"When we got home from church, I tol' Ma I had a sick headache and needed to lay down. I lay there and formulated my plan. As soon as everyone went visitin' (you know we used to do that kinda thing every Sunday—went visitin' to one neighbor or another), I tol' ma I couldn't go. I was too sick. So reluctantly she let me stay home with strict instructions not to leave my bed.

"Like I say, as soon as they left, I snuck out of bed and made a beeline to Theophil's place. Only thing is, that was the place my folks decided to visit that day. I had to sneak around in broad daylight with the whole house full of people and steal that goose back without gettin' caught.

"The good Lord was on my side that day. That goose didn't make a squawk as I gently grabbed him and carried him out of the coop and into the shadows of the treeline. He was probably still in shock from the night before. I ducked and dodged and moved between the trees and the tall grasses of the ditch until I was back at the Kasper Schmidt place.

"Again, the Son was shinin' on me 'cause the house was empty and I could get that goose back in the shed without anyone seein' me.

"I got back home and crawled into bed before Ma and Dad got back. As far as I know, the only people that knew I stole that goose, twice, was Kasper Schmidt, me, and now the three of you."

Jack smiled. "That's a heck of a story, but it still doesn't change my opinion. You were a good boy then, and you're a good man now."

David shifted, a little embarrassed. "Okay, okay, that's enough of my nonesense. Who's gonna keep reading Shadow's stories?"

"I will," chuckled Jack. "I see the next few pages look like they're about a conversation between me and my Ma. This should be fun."

As Jack started started to read and remember his family's dinner conversation following the arrival of Kermit and Pius, he laughed. He said he didn't really remember all the details, but it all sure sounded familiar to him. As he read how Hulda offered to teach Clara how to make her white frosted cake and seeing his name and his words recited in my text, his deep and steady voice cracked a little.

"Well, I'll be, Shadow. Reading this makes me remember how it felt to be that smart aleck little boy again. I feel a little strange reading this stuff about my ma out loud. I'm almost afraid she's going to open that door and walk in here to tell me to straighten up and quit talking nonsense about her."

As Jack said this, the other two men chuckled uncomfortably. As I turned from the counter to look at Jack's face, I could see what David and Elmer saw. Jack's mouth had started to quiver, and his eyes were welling with tears. I walked over to him and put my hand on his shoulder. At that moment, this grown man, this leader of the community, this man of the cloth turned into a little boy again and buried his face in the folds of my skirt. I held him close and gently stroked his back. Elmer and David looked down at their hands as Jack worked to get control over his emotions again.

Finally, he sat up. "I swear sometimes I miss that woman more than I can bear. She always saw right through me and didn't let me get by with anything."

He looked from one of us to the other and apologized. "I'm sorry about that. I'm a seventy-year-old man acting like I'm six. You'd think being a pastor, I'd have learned how to control my emotions. But I guess it's true what they say. You never get over the loss of your mother."

David looked his friend in the eyes. "It's a good thing to have emotions, my friend. Hulda wasn't my mother, but I was on the receivin' end of her scoldin' on more'n one occasion. I don't believe anyone truly gets over a woman like that. I find myself thinkin' about her pretty often. I'm always wonderin' what she would say about this or that. Brings a smile to my face every time! She was somethin'. "

"So, Elmer," Jack finally said, "I think it's up to you to read about these two guys."

"OK, Revrand," he replied, "I'll do my best, but ya know I ain't no orator like you."

"You'll do just fine," David reassured him.

As Elmer read the story, I finished the dessert and began to plate it. When he was done reading, I was just turning to put the first two plates on the table.

"Ha!" Jack exclaimed with a smile. "You made Ma's famous white frosted cake!"

I smiled and nodded. I often hear Hulda in my head as well. She was a hard woman, but there was something about her that drew a person to her. I heard someone say once that she was all bark with no bite. I think that describes it pretty well. Tasting her white frosted cake always makes me miss her a little less—like she's not really gone.

"What the heck!" Elmer drawled. "So this is the famous white frosted cake? My granma and ma were always trying to bake it just like Hulda did. We musta ate a hunerd white cakes at the house, but granma swore none of 'em were right. Now this is a treat! I can't wait to tell the wife 'bout this!"

"Ma was pretty protective about her recipes. This Clara woman didn't know how lucky she was that Ma offered to show her. She should have taken her up on it. I don't even think she showed Regina how to make it, did she, Shadow?" Jack asked with a smirk.

I grinned back at him and shook my head, no. I could still see the eyes of that rambunctious boy when he talked about his mother. He understood that only I knew how to make this cake because I'd watched and helped her make it so many times. And she knew I would never tell anyone the recipe, of course.

As they ate their cake (two slices each) and drank their coffee, they discussed Kermit and Pius, each lending a theory about how they got lost in the blizzards and why they found themselves on the train tracks. It was easy to imagine those harsh winters with the way the wind continued to blow outside.

Soon, the conversation drifted to my little house and all of the furniture in it. It was a comfortable, solid little house. Thanks to David, Jack, and all of those at the church, it has been well taken care of.

Elmer asked, "You still got that table? The one with that heart on it?"

I nodded, and as I walked into the living room, I waved for them to join me. I set the lamp on the floor and lifted the crocheted lace doily. I pointed at the spot, and there it was, as plain as the day Pius first showed us: "Jared Loves Lally."

Elmer stood up with his arms folded behind the bib of his overalls. "Ain't that somethin.'"

"Well, gents, I think we best figure out how we're gonna sleep tonight," Jack said as he gazed out of the living room window. "By the look of it, I don't think we'd make it outta the driveway even if we wanted to."

"I'm all for that. It's almost eleven o'clock. These days I'm usually in bed by nine. I just might turn into a pumkin," David joked.

"What the heck!" Elmer interjected with a grin. "We ain't goin' to bed until we finish Shadow's story. You old duffers better look alive. We're almost to the end here."

David chuckled. "Hey, hey, there's no reason for name callin'."

"I fully intend to finish that story tonight, you young pup. I was just thinking we should get our blankets and such settled so we can crawl under the covers as soon as we're done. We gotta be prepared so Shadow can tuck us in like the old days," Jack teased with a wink in my direction.

David laughed. "You fellas should speak for yourselves. She never babysat me, and I don't think I'm inclined to let her start tonight."

Hearing them, I was suddenly a little anxious because I realized for the first time that night that I only had two beds in the house, and one of them was mine. Where would I put these men? I can count on one hand the number of overnight guests I've had over the years. I was sure I didn't have enough pillows and blankets, either.

Elmer started walking to the front door and grabbed his coat and boots.

David stood watching him perplexed. "You fixin' to go somewhere, Elmer?"

"We gonna need some blankets, not? I'm just gonna run out to the truck and grab the bed roll I keep shoved behind the seat in case I get stuck out in the weather."

"Good thinking, Elmer. Actually, I have a thick blanket and a pillow in the back seat of my car. The kids are always sleeping back there when we go to the city," Jack added.

Elmer had his boots, coat, hat, and gloves on. "No need for all of us to go out in this weather. Why don't you stay here where it's warm and let this 'pup' go get the beddin'. You got anythin' in your vehicle you want me to bring in, David?"

"Ya, there's an old wool blanket behind the seat. You sure you don't want help?"

"I think I can handle it."

When Elmer opened the door, I was shocked at how much snow had drifted up already. It was almost a third of the way up the door. Because of the cold, the snow was very light and fluffy, but it was falling extremely hard. I couldn't even see the vehicles in the driveway that were only a few yards away. In the short time the door was open, a wind gust blew a surprising amount of snow into the foyer.

Elmer didn't hesitate to go out in the elements, though. He plodded right outside and closed the door behind him. He made his way through the knee-deep snow to his truck and then Jack's car. He was quite a sight when he eventually kicked at the door for us to let him in. Between the snow and the blankets, he was hardly visible.

As he turned to go back out to get David's blanket, I put my hand on his elbow to stop him. I shook my head and pointed upstairs. David saw what I was doing and started laughing. "Elmer, she's trying to tell you not to go back out in that storm. I forgot. She's got two rooms upstairs. I can just stay in the guest room."

"I'll take the floor down here, then," offered Elmer. "You can have the sofa, Jack."

"Well, you don't have to offer that twice. I'll take it."

As the men laid out their blankets and gathered some pillows from the furniture, I started making some sweet rolls for breakfast. I use a yeast dough and like to let it rise overnight.

Once again, the men gathered around the kitchen table as I stood at the counter preparing the next meal. I have to say, I was enjoying the evening immensely. There is very little I appreciate more than feeding hungry mouths. Listening to them read my stories and reminisce truly warmed my soul.

As I started to mix and knead the dough, I recalled a little spat Jack and Hulda had years before. Jack was probably twelve or thirteen by then and still getting under her skin at every turn. I don't remember what they argued about the night before, but the next morning when Hulda put his plate of eggs, bacon, and toast in front of him, we all knew something was up.

We always could sense the tension in the house when those two were annoyed with each other. If there was any doubt that day, it was removed the moment we heard the plate drop in front of Jack with a huff.

Jack took his fork, scooped up some of the egg, and dropped it on the edge of his toast. Then he picked up the piece and took a big mouthful. After he swallowed, he complained, "Geez Ma, I can't hardly eat this breakfast."

"What do you mean?"

"There is no flavor in these eggs. You didn't make them with love this morning, and I can taste it."

"What in Heaven's name are you talkin' about, Jack? I made those eggs the same way I do every morning. Now hush up and eat your breakfast."

"No, thank you. You're mad at me, and I can taste it. I'll just take this apple and eat it on the way," he announced as he got up from the table, grabbed his books, and left the house for school.

I remember being nervous as the door closed behind him. It was quiet for a bit, and I wasn't sure if Hulda would go running after him or tell me to. In the end, Herman started grinning and all at once he, Regina, and the boys were laughing so hard they were crying. Hulda tried to resist, but it didn't take long before she was shaking her head and laughing right along with them.

If I recall it right, Hulda made Jack the same cinnamon rolls the next morning that I was making that night. Cinnamon and sugar have always been a weakness for Jack, and when it's baked in a yeast dough with a heavy layer of powdered sugar frosting on top, he couldn't resist.

As he shoveled his third helping into his mouth the following day, he managed to announce, "Now this tastes like love, Ma!"

Hulda's house was strict and orderly, but there's no doubt that it was filled with love. As I finished the dough and set it on the counter, I wondered if Jack remembered that morning. I know I think of it almost every time I make these rolls.

I was about to start another pot of coffee when David stopped me. "Shadow, I can't speak for these two, but I gotta switch to plain water. If I take in anymore of that strong coffee, I won't sleep for a week."

The other two nodded in agreement, so I just finished prepping. I cleaned the flour off the counter and covered the bowl with a flour sack cloth. The one I pulled out of the drawer was embroidered with a little poodle wearing a funny hat. The edges were trimmed in a reddish orange thread that matched the flower in the dog's hat. It was one that Regina had made for me when I moved into my little house. I don't know why she chose such a silly image, but it has always been one of my favorites.

"Looks like she titled this next bit 'Regina,'" David remarked as he grabbed the pile of papers. "We're going to hear about your sister, Jack."

"Well, that's going to be a nice education for me as well! I can't say I remember her very well when she was a young girl. You know, Regina was five years older than me and never wanted much to do with me. I got to know her better when I went out to Washington those two summers in my late teen, but I mostly hung around with the neighbor kids. They treated me like I was some exotic pet from the country."

David laughed. "Yes, I recall that now. My ma remarked once, 'Hulda put Jack on the train again this morning. Herman says it does them all good for the two of them to take a break from each other over the summers."

Jack grinned. "Ya, Ma and I really knew how to get under each other's skin. And with three older brothers and me so much younger, I really wasn't needed to help much with the farming. I spent most of my time with my head in a book. I liked going out West, and I think Regina liked having someone around to keep Adeline company, too. Regina and Ignatz worked some awfully long hours at their little store."

Elmer interjected, "We best get readin' if we're gonna finish before mornin', not?"

"Now who's getting tired?" David asked with a smirk.

Elmer leaned back in his chair. His arms folded in the bib of his striped overalls. "Yep. I ain't gonna deny it. It's late for all of us, not?"

With that, David began reading what I'd written about Regina, Siegfried, Johanna and their girls named after flowers, the plague, and their eventual deaths.

"I never heard any a this before," Elmer remarked. "That is one sad story. You still tendin' to the graves of those girls, Shadow?"

By this time I'd finished with the breakfast prep and took my place at the table. My eyes met Elmer's as I nodded. In truth, I don't know how long I'll be able to keep up my visits to the cemetery, but I did make it out there at least twice last year. Once in the spring and then again in the fall. The flowers had grown and spread to the point that there wasn't much maintenance needed. Only a few weeds managed to make their way through their mature root systems.

Jack said, "I can't say I heard much about this family either. Regina was gone a lot, but I never knew she was with Johanna and her girls. I heard stories about the plague, of course. I knew there was a newspaper in town, and I think I remember hearing about how the Blue Death wiped out a whole family, but none of it really seemed real before. You know how you hear about starving kids in Africa, but you really don't relate it to your every day life 'cause it's so far away and it's hard to imagine they're real people until you see their faces in those commercials on the TV."

The others around the table nodded.

"Well, I sure do remember those girls," David declared. "The oldest girl, Rose, was just a few years younger than me. She showed up in school, and us boys thought we were dreamin'. We were a little young to be be chasin' girls, and she was too young to chase anyways, but she sure was pretty.

"Thinkin' back on it, you could say we almost abused her. One of us was always tuggin' at her hair or untyin' one of the ribbons that held it in place. We stole her pencils and even threw little pebbles at her. Anythin' a young boy could think of to do to get a pretty little girl's attention, we did.

"The girls in school didn't seem to like her, either. They were always talkin' 'bout how she was puttin' on airs and thought she was better'n them. It was a shame, really, lookin' back. Kids can be cruel."

After a short pause in the conversation, David continued. "I remember one day, we were all sittin' in the classroom. You know, back then it was just a one-room schoolhouse and all the grades sat together. The teacher would work with one group, and while they were doing some exercise, she'd start lecturin' another group."

"It was the same when I went to school," Jack said.

"I sometimes forget just how old you two are. I 'spose next you're gonna start tellin' us 'bout how you had to fight off dinosaurs on your way to the well to fetch the water, huh?" Elmer teased.

David chuckled. "All right, enough of that, you pup."

"Anyway, as I was sayin'," David continued, looking at Elmer with a mock scolding face. "I remember all of us sittin' in class waiting for the music teacher to come in. We were preparing for the annual school program, and she was trying to coerce a melody out of us tone-deaf lot. But that day, before she started rehearsal, she asked Rose to come to the front of the class. Rose got up and timidly went forward.

"The teacher said, 'Okay, just like we practiced.' Then she hummed out a note on her harmonica thing, and all at once Rose opened her mouth and sang 'Silent Night' in such a clear and powerful voice that it snapped us all to attention. The sound that came out of that little girl's mouth was nothing short of miraculous. I swear it darn near brought me to tears, it was so beautiful.

"Some of the girls were a little nicer to her for a few days, but us boys just seemed to increase the torment in our attempts to get her attention. I wonder if we would've been so cruel to her if we would've known how short her life was gonna be?"

"I think there's a sermon in there somewhere," Jack thought aloud. "I might use that story one of these Sundays, if you don't mind."

"Be my guest. Just don't point to me when you talk about the tormentor." David winked. "Why don't you take over the readin' for a while, Jack?"

"Sure."

As Jack continued to read about how Regina got herself into trouble and the circumstances that brought Adeline into the world, I started wringing my hands.

These are things that weren't talked about back then and aren't talked about now. Getting pregnant out of wedlock is still a disgrace to the family. Not to mention a mother trying to give her child away to passing strangers.

I was pretty sure Jack wouldn't like that I wrote this part down in black and white. I suddenly felt so ashamed. What was I thinking? I couldn't look up. I couldn't look any of them in the eyes. As Jack read about his sister, I sat staring at my hands, quietly weeping.

When Jack finished, the room fell very quiet. Then, with a deep sigh, David whispered, "What the hell, Shadow? Why would you write this? Regina was like a sister to you. You even wrote in these pages that you felt like she was a sister. Why would you put this scandal in black and white? You're probably the only person that knew any of this. You could've taken it to your grave! What point did writing this down have?" Then, he turned to Jack who had sat in a stunned silence since putting down the final page. "I'm sorry, Jack. You shouldn't have had to hear that, much less read it."

I still sat with my head down, feeling the weight of my friend's words hang in the air. I've spent my whole life in silence. Why did I feel compelled to write all these secrets now?

Quietly, Jack cleared his throat and put a hand on David's arm. "David, Shadow wrote this because it's true. It happened, and I think it's important that things like this get talked about."

Elmer shifted uncomfortably. "I'm sorry, Jack, but I have to go along with David on this one. A story like this should be kept quiet, not?"

Jack said, "Shadow, look at me. It's okay."

I lifted my head but could barely see his face through my guilty tears.

"Shadow, I've heard rumors about this my whole life. Heck, Adeline herself told me most of them. I've thought about this often over the years. When Regina got herself into trouble, it was a bad time for all of us. The town shunned the lot of us. The gossip was relentless. Us boys were tormented almost every day as one and then another of our friends made comments about our sister.

"I surprised my dad in the barn one day after school. His head was leaning against the stall door and he was crying. It was the only time in my whole life I saw tears in my father's eyes. It was the day after ma told us that Regina was pregnant."

David interrupted. "It sounds like you're provin' my point, Jack. My uncle always said, 'Don't go kickin' a dog turd once it's stopped stinkin'.' Shadow just kicked up a big ol' turd by writin' this down. Even if it is true."

"But that's just it, David. She shined a light on something here. This kind of gossip and shaming must stop. It's not up to us to judge; it's up to the Lord. Imagine how tormented my sister must have been to be brought to the point of giving away her own daughter. The loneliness, pettiness, and just plain meanness that she endured was unnecessary and proved no point. Regina made a mistake. As Shadow so eloquently wrote, she was grief-stricken and sought comfort the only way she could find it. If someone would have shown her compassion and understanding, maybe she wouldn't have felt so alone. Maybe she wouldn't have looked for refuge in the arms of a man. But, once she did, if she had been loved, supported, and helped, think how things would have been different."

"Well, I can see why you're such a good minister," Elmer said, shaking his head. "You really believe what you preach."

"You bet I do. I'm glad Shadow wrote this down. I think there's more than just one sermon in that story. I might just use it for a confirmation lesson. I could call it, 'And, the greatest of these is Love.'"

"I'm still not so sure I would want a story like this about my family gettin' out, but I guess if you're not mad, I got no reason to be upset," David conceded.

I couldn't believe what I was hearing. These men weren't mad after all. I looked at Jack. I tried to convey to him just how sorry I was for bringing this all up again. How ashamed I was for even remembering it, much less putting it all down on paper.

Jack looked deep into my eyes. "Fellas, I owe Shadow a great debt. There isn't anything she could ever do that would make me upset with her. She has a kind and loving heart where no malice could ever hide.

"When I was a boy, I got in a lot of trouble. Well, there's proof enough of that in the pages that sit in front of us, isn't there? I would often seek Shadow out to tell her my woes. I told her everything. I bared my soul to her. If I felt it, thought it, or wished it, I shared it. Shadow has been my counselor, but even more than that. She's been a guiding light.

"Shadow may not speak with words, but I know you both will agree when I say she speaks volumes with her eyes."

"Well, I can't argue with that!" David replied.

"There was more than one occasion when I was heading down a wrong path, and she gave me a look that set me right again." He looked at me. "C'mon, Shadow, don't look so surprised. You know what I'm talking about."

I lowered my eyes.

He continued, "Well, remember when I told you I was homesick and went to the chapel to pray—and that's where I got my calling?"

We all nodded.

"I went to that chapel because I knew it would be quiet. I needed to talk to my Shadow, and I was hundreds of miles away from her. I figured the next best thing would be to try talking to God. Maybe He could set me on the right path until I could get home.

"Don't you see, Shadow? Because of you, I found my calling. Because of you, I found God!"

He turned to the others. "No, sir, there's nothing this woman could ever do or say that would make me feel anything but blessed that she was a part of my life! Now, I'm tired. Let's get some sleep!"

Without another word, each of those men stood and one by one kissed the top of my head before they made their way to bed.

The next morning I woke slowly to the sound of movement in the house below. It startled me for a brief moment until I remembered I had overnight guests. As the sleepy haze left my mind, I realized that I needed to get up and get breakfast going. What kind of hostess sleeps later than the men? I could just hear Hulda's scolding tone.

I quickly dressed and scurried down the stairs to find Jack and Elmer putting their winter coats and boots on. "Mornin', Shadow," Elmer whispered. "Hope we didn't wake you. Jack and me figure we better get a start on clearin' that snow, or else we may need to spend another night."

As Jack opened the door, I couldn't help but gasp. The snow had drifted about two thirds of the way up the door. I've seen big snows over the years, but nothing like that.

The warmth of the house seemed to suck the cold, crisp air inside. The wind had died down, and through the slit at the top of the opening, you could see the sun beginning to come up.

The men kicked and punched their way through the door like a couple of ten-year-old boys. *Giggling* was the only word that would accurately describe their laughter as they tumbled out of the house. The winter air and promise of the wakening sunshine seemed to have lifted their spirits as much as it did mine.

Such joy to have loved ones bringing energy into the home!

I quickly turned the oven to preheat while I rolled the dough flat. I mixed the cinnamon, sugar, and butter into a paste and spread it on the surface. Just as Hulda had taught me, I gently rolled the sheet of pastry so the filling created the perfect spiral when I sliced the log into the individual rolls. I put them in a pan and set it on the stove top to let the heat of the oven help move the final rise along.

As I waited for the dough to be ready for the oven, I gathered the rest of the food for breakfast. I sliced some of the summer sausage one of the neighbors dropped off after deer season. I usually prefer pork to venison, but this batch was from a young doe, so it didn't taste gamey.

I also grabbed a package of soda crackers and set out the head cheese and liver sausage that was in the back of the ice box. If there is one thing I learned growing up in Hulda and Herman's home, it's that men like meat, especially after physical labor like clearing snow.

I sliced some bread and started toasting it. I spread each piece with a generous pat of butter when it was still hot. The melted butter soaks into the bread and makes it so delicious when you add some raspberry or plum jelly on top. I had both kinds, so I set those out as well.

As I was fussing with the breakfast, David came down the stairs and gave me a one-armed hug. He smiled, "It smells good down here. The other two must be hard at it already, huh?"

I nodded and grabbed a cup for him. As I set it down at his place at the table, I realized I hadn't made a pot yet. I motioned my dilemma, and he assured me, "Don't worry, Shadow. I need to get out there and help dig us out anyway."

He started to dress for the outdoors, and after he put his hat on, he turned to me. "Um, I need to tell you that I'm sorry for my behavior last night. I lashed out at you, and it wasn't fair. You didn't do anything wrong, and even if you did, it wasn't up to me to say anything. I feel just awful. Shadow, can you forgive me?"

David's apology was so heartfelt. I could feel my eyes start to well up as I fought back the tears. I nodded and gave him a slight smile then a little shrug to let him know there was nothing to forgive.

He nodded and opened the door to go out. By now the sun was fully up and shining, so bright it almost hurt my eyes as it reflected off the white snow. It was breathtakingly beautiful. Everything was clean and sparkling. It looked as if the world was covered in diamonds.

Jack and Elmer had made good progress on the sidewalk and were starting to dig out the vehicles. "Nice of you to join us, sleepy head!" Jack teased.

David shut the door, so I could only hear their muffled conversation as I mopped up the melted snow from the floor and got back to making breakfast.

After I put the rolls in the oven, I remembered I had a couple potatoes and an onion in the bucket I keep on the back porch. I got them frying and cracked a few eggs to scramble. Then I mixed the frosting so it would be ready when the rolls were cool enough. Finally, I made that pot of coffee.

By the time I'd prepared the food and set the table, I heard some rustling at the door. The men had done enough to free their vehicles and were coming in to warm up. Perfect timing.

Elmer said, "We can get out now, not? After breakfast I'll run home and get the blade on my truck. Once I get my place cleared, I can come back and finish the job here."

"Sounds like a winner to me," David agreed. "I 'spect Jack and me will have plenty more to clear at our places as well."

"Goodness, what a feast this is!" Jack exclaimed as they all took their seats at the table. "The way you've been spoilin' us, I'm not sure we'll ever leave!"

I poured us all a hot cup of coffee and sat down to eat.

Jack said a short prayer, and everyone started to pass the food and fill their plates.

In between bites, David said, "Shadow, I apologized to you this morning for my angry comments last night, but there's something else I need to share.

"In those stories we read last night, you made it sound like you weren't important or that you didn't matter because you don't speak. It bothered me all night. I want you to know that your silence has meant more to me throughout my life than any words I ever heard spoken."

I pursed my lips and shook my head. He didn't have to say that nonesense.

"I'm being serious here, now, Shadow. When I was a boy and had problems at home or at school, I came to you to talk it out. When I met Doris and was too shy to ask her to go walkin' with me, I came to you to talk through my anxiety. When I wanted to ask her to marry me, I practiced with you. Remember?"

I nodded and smiled. Of course I remembered.

"When I bought the dealership, when the stock market crashed, when the babies started comin', you were the first person I wanted to tell. Heck, I'm almost eighty-years-old, and the day my wife died, the first thing I did was head over here. I truly don't know how I would've gotten through that without you."

I was stunned. I didn't expect this, and I had to look away. I know he liked to talk things over with me, but I always thought he talked like that with everyone.

Before David could start talking again, Elmer interrupted. "I was up thinking along those same lines last night, too. Shadow, I owe you a debt of gratitude I don't think I could ever repay."

I gave him a confused look. My first thought was that he was enjoying the breakfast, but there was nothing special on this table.

He continued. "You two don't know this, but when me and the wife were married about a year, she got pregnant. We figured she was only about a month or two along when she told me. Well, we both wanted a big family just like the ones we grew up in, so this was more than welcome news. I was so happy I was 'bout to burst, but the wife said it was bad luck to tell anyone 'fore she was three months along, so I kept it to myself.

"A couple weeks later, the wife got up in the middle of the night and started screaming for me to come into the bathroom. There was a lot of blood, and we both knew right away that she'd lost the baby. I took her into town and had the doctor take care of her. Once we got home, she settled into bed and fell into a fitful sleep.

"I didn't know what to do. I never felt so sad and lost in my whole life. She kept saying, 'I'm sorry. I'm sorry.' Like it was her fault or somethin'. Well, as she slept, I came over here. I knocked on that door, and when I saw Shadow's face, I busted out cryin' like a little kid.

"I knew I wouldn't have to say anything or explain anything or try to be strong. Shadow just looked at me and took my hand. She led me to that sofa and sat down with my head in her lap as I sobbed.

"Once I got it all outta my system, I told her what happened, and she just sat with me. Quiet. She didn't say it was gonna be all right or that it was God's will. She just sat and listened and comforted. It's just what I needed.

"When I got home, I felt strong enough to be a comfort to my wife. I was able to do for her just what Shadow had done for me. I was able to quietly comfort her."

"Elmer, I had no idea. I'm sorry," Jack said.

David had been looking down at the table this whole time. He lifted his head and looked at me. With a voice that cracked as he spoke, he said, "You matter, Shadow. You matter."

Acknowlegements

I may have written the words on these pages but I wouldn't have been able to finish a complete sentence without a great deal of help and support.

I want to thank my father, Richard, for his strong and steady guidance throughout my life. He is one of the best storytellers I know and supplied me with many of the ideas for this book. My mother, Gurine, always had a way of making me believe that I was special and could accomplish whatever I set my mind to. Without their love and support, I would never have had the courage to begin.

My uncle Elmer taught me the joy of sharing a story and how to add just enough to it to make people laugh. He never completely made anything up, he just added a bit here and there to make it interesting.

I've been blessed to have hosted six exchange students, Daniel, Haris, Tabraiz, Daniyar, Anthony and Enrico. Each helped me to broaden my view of the world and the people in it. I especially want to thank Daniel who will recognize himself in several of the characters in this book. Also, I wouldn't have kept going without Haris's constant encouragement which actually felt more like bullying at times.

The Night Writers writing group provided me with insight and suggestions that allowed me to write the way I wanted to while using my own voice. Because of their skill, talent and insights, this story became more than just words on paper.

Mostly, I want to thank the love of my life, my best friend and husband, Scott. Marrying him was the single best decision of my life. He has always been my biggest fan and has stood by me throughout it all.

I started this book as a way to ensure the stories of our family would survive the generations. It was written for you, Paul, Tom, Ariela, Jon, Logan, Skipper and Chance.

www.ingramcontent.com/pod-product-compliance
Lightning Source LLC
Chambersburg PA
CBHW030533270626
47155CB00024B/3031